I0727321

Broken Dreams:

A Paranormal Protector Tale

Book 3 in the Heart of Stone series

DEMELZA CARLTON

This book was created with the assistance a grant from the Western Australian Department of Local Government, Sport and Cultural Industries.

DEDICATION

This one is for all the amazing staff and volunteers at Fremantle Prison, for their help (and patience) while I was researching this series. You do an amazing job, and I can't thank you enough.

ONE

"I declare you guilty of the murder of Lady Pamela Burke, and sentence you to be hanged by the neck until dead."

For any normal man, or any murderer, those words should have signalled the end of his story.

But for Ben and his brothers, who were not guilty of Pamela's murder, no matter what the magistrate said, it was but the beginning of a new chapter, a twist in the tale, as it were, because in Ben's experience, fate always had other plans.

As did the prison Superintendent.

"I do not like that shirt. The collar points are too high, and my cravat is tied all wrong for the current fashion. I insist you change it, more like so." The Superintendent lifted his chin so that Ben might better see how his cravat was tied today.

Ben nodded gravely. "Yes, sir. But I will need a new canvas and more paint, to properly capture your likeness anew. As always, I am at your service, sir." He bowed deeply, almost like a gentleman, or perhaps a gentleman's valet, though he was neither.

"Then you shall have it. I must have a portrait that portrays me perfectly." The Superintendent rang the bell with violence more in keeping with his reputation as the hard man in charge of a prison filled with the worst offenders in Scotland. "Alan!" he bellowed.

Alan, the Superintendent's manservant, appeared after a short moment. "Yes, sir?" He pointedly ignored Ben, as usual. Prisoners were beneath his notice.

"I want you to order more canvas and

paints for Stone here. Immediately!" the Superintendent said.

"Yes, sir." His bow wasn't as low as Ben's had been, which made the Superintendent frown. "Forgive me, sir, but a messenger arrived with an urgent letter." Alan held out the missive, his thumb carefully placed over the wax seal so as to hide it from Ben's view.

Ben hid a smile. He didn't care a whit for the Superintendent's correspondence, but he'd hear about it soon enough, for the man liked to talk while Ben painted. Usually about the latest fashions in London, for the man was definitely a dandy of the most passionate kind, but on rare occasions, he talked of other things.

Sure enough, the Superintendent snatched the letter from his servant's hand and dismissed him. Ben added a few brushstrokes to his painting while he waited, knowing that the Superintendent would change his mind on the morrow, and wish to keep this one as well as anything else he commanded Ben to create.

Finally, the Superintendent made a derisive sound and threw the letter down on the table.

"Do you know what foolishness the high and mighty in London are up to this time?"

Some strange, new fashion, most likely. Ben allowed his eyes to widen in surprise. "Me? No, sir."

"They seem to think that there are good men in prison, hard workers, and not just criminals. They want me to find any man trained in the building trades – stonemasonry, brickwork, carpentry, and the like – so they might transport them to the Swan River Colony to build things!"

This was definitely an improvement over the latest way to tie a cravat. Hope gave a feeble flap within Ben's breast. "Indeed, sir?"

The Superintendent laughed. "They have even offered a reward for every felon transported." He grew thoughtful. "Do you know of any prisoners who might satisfy my superiors? Even one man?"

Ben pretended to think hard, then said slowly, "I can only think of three men, sir. My brothers, Torstan and Dunstan, are a master stonemason and a ship's carpenter, respectively, and then there's me. I was training as an apprentice stonemason with my brother Torstan until I was arrested. I would have finished my apprenticeship by now and be a full mason. But I cannot think of any other man who might satisfy you, sir."

The Superintendent's brow furrowed. "But you three are sentenced to hang, and I want my new portrait painted. Then again, there is the reward, and saving the cost of the hangman…"

Ben remained silent. He knew the man's vanity and greed warred for supremacy, but he also knew greed always won, for the more coin the Superintendant had, the more he could pay his tailor.

"I suppose it's a fate worse than death, being sent to the Swan River Colony. I've heard stories of men starving, killed by natives, or wild animals. The soils are so stained in blood, they are permanently red. Nary a woman to be seen, for it is not safe for them, either. With the reward, I might hire a proper painter, too…"

Ben tried to look worried, while his heart soared. Fate was smiling on him, in her twisted way. If he had to choose between working bloodstained foreign soil or rotting in this prison, he wouldn't hesitate. "Oh, sir, that sounds terrible. Perhaps if you were to forget I spoke. I'd much rather stay here than be sent to the Colonies. It sounds positively frightful."

Ah, there it was. The Superintendent's sadistic smile, when he thought he was being particularly cruel. "Then you shall go to the Colonies, Stone. You and your brothers. Perhaps you can pay for your crimes there with your lives instead of being a plague upon good men here. And I shall be able to pay a real painter to paint my portrait."

The Superintendent summoned a guard to take Ben back to his cell. Ben dragged his feet, hanging his head, but secretly, his heart was lighter than air, for his dearest wish was about to be granted.

TWO

When Ben was only a wee lad, his father would take him and his brothers down to the Firth of Clyde, and he'd point out to sea, where the Kintyre peninsula ended, and he'd say that fate awaited them out there. Ben and his brothers would peer out at the Irish Sea, straining their eyes to see through the mists, tasting the salt from the waves rocking the boat beneath them, and he swore he could almost taste the future his father promised. Mother's brother, Uncle Stanley, who had gone to the Swan

River Colony before Ben was born, had sent a letter from those faraway southern shores, and Father would quote from it. How Fremantle was like the cliffs of Dover, white sand and stone, topped with green enough to feed as many sheep and cattle as they could imagine, and on the shore as much seaweed as a man could want to fertilise his fields, just piled up on the beach, waiting for them.

All his life, Ben had wanted to believe Father's tales of this land where fortune waited for them, if they were only bold enough to follow her. Even now, in the predawn light, waiting for the sun to rise over the town of Fremantle so that they'd finally be allowed to go ashore, he dared to hope, even as he told himself it was all a fairy story, the sort of fanciful tale told to children to give them exactly this kind of false hope. Yet when the sun rose over those white buildings, blessing them with her rosy glow, Ben could have sworn he was still dreaming.

The taste of salt stung his cracked lips as he beheld the limestone cliffs, shearing off to his left, while the waves played between the ship and the shore, licking one and then the other, not sure which one it liked the taste of best. If he listened hard, he could even hear the waves whispering to the sand, as they caressed it like an army of lovers, one after the other. The waves might touch the ship, as if forced by duty, but what they really loved was the land.

Just like Uncle Stanley, apparently, or so Father had said.

Just as Ben meant to, if this land would only let him.

It seemed like scarcely a moment before the sun was high in the sky, and he and his brothers were rowing ashore, shoulder to shoulder with the other convicts. For all the stories of being clapped in irons and chain gangs that he'd heard along the way, it was almost like being a free man again, headed home instead of into the unknown.

Until one of the waves splashed over the side of the boat and the water was warm. Back home, the sea would be near freezing, but here…here it was like a bath. Stanley had been right, then. The Swan River Colony truly was paradise.

But convicts were not meant to enjoy the view – they were here to work, the guards reminded them as they ordered them to unload the boats and carry the cargo into the three-storey warehouse on the edge of the beach.

Inside the warehouse, the floor was damp beach sand, littered with seaweed, but the guards wanted the convicts to carry the cargo inside, and lay them on top of the other soaked sacks and chests. For while the warehouse walls might be finished outside, there was nothing inside – no floors or walls or stairs.

Tor and Dunstan did not approve, muttering under their breath about the foolishness of bringing anything in here, only to have it ruined, when it was clear from the timber and ballast stacked outside, ready to be loaded aboard ships, that things would be safer outside, beneath the cloudless skies. Ben listened to them for long enough to know what they thought they should do, before he caught the eye of one of the guards he'd helped in the shipboard school.

"Sir, do you know why this warehouse is not finished?" Ben asked as he passed, careful not to break stride as he lifted a sack onto each shoulder and carried them off the beach.

"Not enough labour, lad. That's what you're here for," the guard said.

Ben nodded thoughtfully. "So that's why my brothers were talking about using that timber to build stairs and upper levels, and those ballast flagstones to raise the floor above the sand." He pulled a pencil and notepad from his pocket and began to sketch what Dunstan had described. "Something like this, sir?" With a few lines, he was done, and he tore off the page to hand it to the guard.

Ben had dallied too long – one of the Colony guards had noticed, and was headed over to chastise him for slowing in his work. The other guard quickly hushed him, and showed him the sketch, as Ben hurried to lift another sack.

By nightfall, they'd begun winching sacks from the sand up to the boards on Dunstan's newly constructed landing. By the end of the week, the landing was a complete first floor, with a second underway, and Tor had started laying Yorkshire flagstones on the sand below.

He'd even heard Mr Henderson suggesting to Mr Wray, his first officer, that they might even be able to extend the Commissariat according to the original plans, if the productivity continued at this pace. For that was the fancy name of the warehouse, which towered over most of the other buildings in Fremantle, with the exception of the Round House, at the top of the cliffs at Arthur Head.

So when Ben lay down beside his brothers, all in their hammocks strung up in a row in the much less salubrious warehouse known as Scott Buildings, a short distance along the beach, he had the satisfaction of knowing that they might be convicts, but they were helping to construct the Swan River Colony, and on their way to earning a ticket of leave or perhaps even a pardon, when they'd be free to seek out their own fortunes, exactly as Father had dreamed, all those years ago. In the meantime, he meant to keep his head down and do as he was told. At least he retired with a bellyful of bread and soup every night, which was more than he'd had in the prison in Scotland. And while hanging by the neck until dead was still a threat, when he lay in his hammock in the warm night air, the chill grasp of death around his throat seemed as distant as faraway Scotland.

THREE

"I can help you escape," a soft voice said, though it carried all the way across the road, for the man who must have spoken stood before a butcher's shop with his arms folded across his apron, clearly the proprietor of the place.

Ben's brothers ignored him – Dunstan because he was too busy trying to keep Tor on his manacled feet, while Tor swayed, blood from last night's lashes seeping through his particoloured slops. As if the lashing wasn't punishment enough, he was forced to dress like some medieval jester and work as hard as anyone else, while wearing chains. All for telling the truth, that the prison walls the engineers had designed would fall over in the first winter storm.

Ben should have spoken to the guards instead. Not Torstan. It still might not have done any good – the engineers did not deign to listen to the concerns of mere convicts, master stonemasons or no, but Ben might have saved him the whipping, or the chains.

"I know where there's gold to be found. Gold no one else knows about. Come with me, and you can be rich. Rich enough to buy your passage home, and never work a day in your lives again. No more irons, and no more lash, ever." There was a darkness in the butcher's tone now, as if he recognised Torstan's pain. Perhaps he had – plenty of convicts had been granted a pardon in the last five years. Everyone on Ben's ship had at least earned their ticket of leave. Except the three Stone brothers, still as much prisoners as the day they'd arrived.

"More gold than you can imagine," the butcher crooned, a faraway look in his eyes.

Enough gold to buy their freedom and passage home? Maybe even enough for Ben to pay to learn to paint properly?

Ben shook his head. It was a dream, a false promise. No one else was listening to the butcher – maybe everyone else knew he was a madman who said nothing but nonsense.

"Nonsense," Ben said. "If you had that much gold, why would you share it with anyone? Slavery's illegal, old man, for that's what it would be for anyone who accepted your offer."

"No, I would share it. There is enough for all those who help me protect it. I promise you," the butcher insisted.

"Where is this gold?" Ben challenged him. "Victoria? They don't let convicts in there. You need papers for that."

The butcher shuddered. "No, not Victoria. The gold is here." He stamped his foot on the road, as though it was buried beneath their feet.

"No one's found gold in Western Australia. I'd have heard about it if they had!" Ben scoffed. He would, too. Fremantle was as full of gossip as any village in Scotland.

The butcher laid his finger beside his nose. "Not if it is a secret that only I know." He glanced around, then dropped his voice. "Meet me here at midnight on Sunday night, and I shall show you." He scanned the street one more time, before hurrying inside his shop.

"Ben, what are you doing there? Get over here and help me with Tor. I think he needs to see the prison physician."

Ben dutifully headed back to help Dunstan with their brother. Between them, they hauled him home to his hammock in Scott Buildings, his chains clinking ominously with every step.

FOUR

Sunday dawned bright and sunny, a perfect summer's day if he'd been in Scotland. But it was winter in Fremantle, and the wind had a bite to it. Sadly, not a big enough bite to blow over the walls Tor was still swearing about.

Two of the warders' families were picnicking by the beach, while the older boys waded into the shallows with their fishing rods, declaring they would catch a shark for supper.

Ben considered asking if the boys could fish

somewhere else, or even just ignoring them. His painting was almost finished, anyway. Finally, he decided the boys belonged where they were – both on the beach, and in his painting. It would take longer to finish, but it wasn't like he wanted to go back to Scott Buildings anyway. Better that he work on this commission and enjoy a day in the sun.

Watercolours suited the washed out winter sky, and the ships anchored in Gage Roads, the shipping channel that separated Fremantle from Rottnest Island, which he'd seen as a shadow on the horizon on clear days. Not today. He wished he had oils for the boys, though, to better distinguish one from the other. As it was, they all looked alike, brushed into the landscape in browns, a foreground to the shingle-topped buildings across the bay.

The Commissariat held pride of place, with its blood-red sheoak shingles rising above all others in town. It had been the first building he'd worked on with his brothers, but not the last. They'd built half the town, from the streets up, including the soon to be opened new prison. Not alone, of course – hundreds of other convicts had joined them, before getting their tickets of leave and heading out to find employment elsewhere in the colony.

"That looks lovely," a woman's voice said.

Ben glanced over his shoulder, to find one of the warder's wives standing not an arm's length from him, holding out a cup of tea. He took it, nodding his thanks to the woman.

"I've told John I want him to hang it over the fireplace, so I can see it every day," she continued. "Especially with my boys in it. I never had a painting of my family before. I thought that was just for lords and ladies and things."

Ah, so this was the wife of the warder who'd commissioned the piece. A brave woman, travelling halfway across the world with her husband to start a new life in a new colony. Like Pamela would have, if she'd lived.

Ben sighed. Pamela would have been in raptures, wanting to draw every waking moment she was here. She'd talked of finding gold, too, just like the butcher. Maybe he wasn't so mad, if someone as educated as she was knew gold was to be found here.

If Pamela hadn't died, perhaps he would have come here with her, and their children, to paint and picnic and… If only he'd been home that night, instead of out with his brothers. Maybe he'd have been able to save her. If only…

"We should ask him to paint a wedding portrait of our Vicky, when she gets married," one of the warders said.

"Vicky's only seven! He'll be long gone by the time she weds," his wife scoffed.

"Not this one, or his brothers. Murderers, all three of them. They killed a woman back in Scotland. Right horrible murder it was, had even her lord father in tears when he talked about it before the magistrate, I heard. Men like him are the reason we're building that big new prison, with walls high enough to keep them in, away from our families. Some of the convicts serve their sentence and get pardoned, but the real bad apples like this one will be convicts for life. Can't trust them around normal, law-abiding folk. Don't know why they didn't just hang all of them instead of sending them all the way out here…"

The warder's wife had vanished, no longer brave enough to stand at Ben's side.

Ben closed his eyes. Maybe he'd had enough sun for one day. "The painting is finished, sir," he said. "If you'd like to see it."

The watercolour met with the warden's approval, and the warder was only too happy to take Ben back to the prisoner barracks, where he was issued with extra rations for the work. Ben merely tucked the bundle under his arm and went to find his brothers.

FIVE

The convict barracks were empty but for the Stone brothers, and a guard posted by the door. Ben was surprised for a moment, until he remembered that the rest of the convicts had been sent on work parties out to York or Champion Bay, leaving space for the new shipload of convicts due to arrive any day.

He'd wondered why they hadn't been added to one of the work parties, but now he had his answer: for all his dreams of freedom, and his plans of one day meting out true justice to

Pamela's murderer, he was doomed to die right here within the prison walls he and his brothers had built. He hoped Tor was right about the walls falling down in a storm, because there was no way they'd ever escape from this place otherwise. When the prison was finished, the inside of those walls was all he'd ever see. Forever.

Dunstan had saved some dinner for him, which Ben ate quickly in between telling them what he'd heard at the beach.

"We're going to die here. We've been building our own tomb," Ben finished.

No response. Not one word from either of his brothers.

"Well?" he asked.

Dunstan shrugged. "If I could go back in time, and you'd never looked at that girl…"

"Don't you blame Pamela for this. Even if I'd never met her or spoken a word to her, there's no saying that lying cove wouldn't have killed her anyway and still left her poor body in our house, or in the quarry, or the castle, or somewhere that would have made us look guilty. Maybe if you two hadn't insisted we go out to see that oracle that night, Queen of the Kelpies or whatever she was, we'd have been home, and when she came to us for help, we could have defended her against that bastard, before all four of us took ship for this very colony, as free settlers instead of in chains!" Ben kicked Tor's manacles, which jingled for a moment before they fell silent.

Tor gave a shudder, but said nothing. His eyes were glazed over, unseeing, but he didn't seem to have a fever. Ben looked askance at Dunstan.

"That's our future. They've broken his spirit, and you and me are next," Dunstan said. He sighed deeply, as though he'd already given up, too.

No. Ben would not allow it. "We have to escape. Before they lock us up in that prison forever. Escape while we still can. We should go meet with that butcher tonight. See what he has to offer."

"The madman who was shouting in the street?" Dunstan shook his head. "Don't be a fool."

"We're fools if we stay here, when we have

a chance to escape. How long do you think Tor will last like this? We have to take our chance now, before the walls are finished and they close the gates with us inside." Ben eyed Tor's manacles. "We'll have to get those chains off him, or they'll make too much noise and give us away."

"We can't…"

"What are they going to do to us if they catch us? We're already facing a lifetime in prison, which is no life at all. I say we go see the butcher. At least listen to what he has to say." Ben moved to the window. With only one guard, no one would be watching that. He'd be out the window and over the wall before anyone was the wiser.

"No, wait, I'm coming with you!" Dunstan said.

"Bring Tor, too."

SIX

A candle burned in the butcher shop window, so Ben knocked at the door, which opened at his touch. The butcher was expecting them, then.

"Come down to the cellar." The butcher beckoned from behind the counter. Ben and his brothers had no choice but to follow him down the stairs, and between the shadowy carcasses that hung from the ceiling to…what appeared to be a privy.

The butcher put a finger to his lips before

he lifted up the bench seat to reveal a ladder, leading down into the darkness.

The brothers glanced at each other. A secret chamber beneath a cellar full of death? This did not bode well.

"If the guards come past, searching for you, they will not find you here. I'll be right down after you – I just need to get some refreshments," the butcher said, hurrying away. The sheep carcasses swayed in his wake.

Dunstan shrugged. "I'll go first. Tor, you come next, and if it's safe, Ben, you come down after. If it's not safe…you're the best one to go and fetch the guards."

Because most of the guards believed Ben to be a good lad who'd been led astray by his brothers. If he were to tell the guards something villainous was going on beneath the butcher's shop, he'd actually be believed, instead of lashed or clapped in irons, like Tor or maybe even Dunstan.

Which would be his brothers' fate, if they weren't hanged for trying to escape, even if Ben was let off lightly.

Ben prayed the butcher's offer was genuine,

and their future would hold freedom.

"Ben! Come down!" Dunstan hissed.

But the butcher was almost back. He set his tea tray down on the floor. "Would you take the biscuit tin, while I carry the teapot?"

Ben held out his hand, tucked the biscuit tin under his arm, and proceeded down the ladder. Dunstan could have built better than this rickety thing with his eyes closed, Ben thought as he made his way carefully down the crooked rungs. He was no carpenter, and he could probably do better.

But when he emerged into the cavern below, he began to understand why. The place looked like the bottom of a mineshaft — wooden beams propping up the cut stone ceiling, and holding up the walls. There were even hand and footholds cut into the limestone wall behind the ladder, as though the ladder was a recent addition to the place. Shelves had been cut into the walls, too, to hold dusty boxes, their contents hidden under canvas covers.

Tor and Dunstan sat on the ledge of a waist-high empty shelf, legs dangling, but when the butcher held up the teapot, they sprang into action. They shifted the table in the corner over to their shelf, and dragged a bench along beside it, so they might all sit at table and have tea.

The butcher produced cups from his pocket and proceeded to pour generous servings. Ben set down the biscuit tin so that he might accept his cup.

"Drink, good sirs, and have a biscuit. Fresh from the bakery on Market Street," the butcher said airily, lifting the lid.

Tor and Dunstan helped themselves, but Ben declined. He'd had his fill of them on the picnic by the beach, and they'd left a sour taste in his mouth.

"Tell us about this gold you've found," Ben said, crossing his arms. "Where in Western Australia did you find it?"

The butcher grinned. "Why, it's right here, of course." He reached for one of the boxes and removed what Ben realised was not a cover, but a folded-over sack. "Take a look for yourself." Gold nuggets tumbled out on the table, gleaming in the lantern light.

Dunstan snatched up a fist-sized piece and bit into it, then grinned. "It's gold, all right." He reluctantly set the knobbly nugget back on the table with its fellows.

Ben's gaze swept the table, measuring the size of the sack, before he counted the boxes lined up along the walls. "If they're all full, that has to be close to five hundred pounds of gold! And you found all that here, under your house?"

The butcher tapped his nose. "If the Governor only knew, eh? He'd have you convicts digging up the roads, instead of building them. But that's why I need good stonecutters and carpenters. Strong men who know how to cut stone and shore it up, willing to work hard and keep my secret. Men who are good in a fight, who'll defend my gold like it's their own, because a part of it will be yours. A percentage of all the gold you dig up."

"What kind of percentage?" Ben asked. Usually, it would be Dunstan asking the questions, but since their arrest, his oldest brother had lost some of his spark, along with his heart, if what the man mumbled in his sleep was true. "If we're doing all the work, it seems we should get no less than equal shares in this venture. A quarter share for each of us."

The butcher laughed. "That sounds fair. Let us shake on it." He held out his hand to Ben.

Ben didn't want to take it. No one gave in that easily, not without bargaining. There was something wrong here.

"I would need it in writing," Ben said.

The butcher produced parchment, a pen and ink, and Ben quickly wrote out the simple contract, then signed his name at the bottom, commanding his brothers to do the same, before pushing the paper toward the butcher. "You, too."

William Silas Pearse scratched out his name, then handed the paper back to Ben. "So we have a deal. Let's drink to it, eh?" He seized the teapot and refilled Tor's and Dunstan's mugs. His own and Ben's were still full.

All four of them raised their cups, clinked them together and drank. The tea tasted like tar, bitter as it coated his tongue before burning the back of his throat, all the way down. Ben gritted his teeth and drank it anyway. Tomorrow, he would make sure he was in charge of brewing the tea properly, not this butcher.

Pearse rose from his seat. "I imagine you men might like a good night's sleep before you start work in the morning. The cellar is yours — no guard will think to look for you here."

Ben glanced around. Where did the butcher expect them to sleep? There wasn't even a hammock, or anywhere suitable to hang one. No blankets…it might not be as cold as Scotland, but it was still winter in Fremantle, and the nights did have a chill to them.

But Tor and Dunstan were already stretching out along the shelves, using their small sacks of belongings as pillows. They must be feigning sleep, so the butcher would leave and they could talk. Yes, that was it.

Ben tucked the signed contract into his sketchbook, then buried it deep at the bottom of his sack, before setting it on an empty shelf for his pillow. He'd just lie down for a moment, until the butcher left them alone.

Pearse tipped the contents of his own mug out on the floor – he hadn't drunk any of it,

Ben realised, before collecting the cups and the teapot and heading up the ladder with them. He left the lantern on the table, though.

Ben waited until he could hear the man's footsteps dying away before following him up the ladder. The privy seat lifted easily – if they wanted to escape, they could. Which made no sense, for the butcher had left a whole bag of gold down there with them. With convicts.

Whichever way Ben looked at it, none of this made sense. If there was gold to find in Fremantle, he and his brothers would have dug some up by now. If the nuggets were real, then they hadn't come from here. Maybe that's what the butcher wanted – free convict labour to build tunnels under Fremantle, where they wouldn't find any gold, but would keep digging in hope of it.

Pearse evidently thought they were idiots.

Well, he'd show Pearse was the fool here, not him, or his brothers. One sack of gold would set them up with farming land, just like they'd wanted. Perhaps not here, where their faces were too familiar, but maybe in Adelaide, or one of the other eastern colonies.

"Dunstan," Ben hissed, shaking his brother's shoulder. Dunstan only snored louder. He didn't wake.

Nor did Tor, even when Ben shouted in his ear.

That's when drowsiness began to steal his wits, too, and he realised there must have been something in the tea. The tea Pearse had not drunk at all.

Cursing, Ben barely made it to his makeshift bed before the drugged tea dragged him down into the darkness.

SEVEN

Rochelle took a deep breath. She was going to finish editing this footage, then submit the assignment, for which she'd get top marks, so she'd definitely pass this unit and all her others so that she could finally, finally finish her degree and graduate at the end of the year.

The power of positive thinking. Or was it the laws of attraction? She'd listened to enough podcasts telling her how to turn her luck around. Surely she was due some good luck soon.

Right. She tapped the icon for her video editing software.

FILE NOT FOUND.

"You'd better be bloody joking. Not again…"

She dug into the menu, looking for it in her list of recent files. Yes, that was the last file she'd worked on. She tapped the file name.

FILE NOT FOUND.

She'd done everything right. Saved it in the cloud drive, backed it up on her laptop, even kept backups of the unedited footage, but they were gone. Even running a search on her hard drive came up with nothing.

"FUCK!"

"Please, no swearing in the background. I'm about to go live, and you know if there's too much swearing, I'll get another community standards violation. If I get too many of those, they'll ban my channel, and we'll lose all our sponsors and ad revenue, and have to start over."

Yes, she did know that. He'd told her often enough. "Sorry, Jakob. It's just that the video files for my assignment are all gone."

A loud, dramatic sigh came from the spare bedroom, which Jakob had set up as his computer den. "It's Iago, babe. Don't use my real name when I'm working."

Yes, because the world would end if his teenage fans discovered he had a name as ordinary as Jakob. Or they might track down his address, and come banging on the front door, fangirling and demanding autographs. Or they might simply get confused, and stop watching, which meant less ad revenue and financial ruin and other such things.

"Sorry. I'm just…upset. I can't find any of my files. Can you take a look? You're the computer whiz, after all. I'm hopeless – as evident by my managing to lose my assignment again, days before it's due."

Jakob – she couldn't think of him as Iago, even if she was supposed to call him that – gave her a pitying look. "Not when I'm about to go live, babe. They dropped a whole heap of new content today, and my fans are dying to hear my take on it as I show it to them for the first time. They're counting on me."

Which meant she couldn't count on him

helping her at all, because after he was done playing games and broadcasting it on his channel, he'd stay on to argue with anyone who commented until the early hours of the morning, before he finally went to bed and slept until after noon, when he'd wake up and start this all over again.

She had no choice but to go and see her lecturer to ask for an extension. If she took in her laptop and actually showed him that the files were missing, maybe…

Who was she kidding? She was going to fail this unit like all the others, and then they'd kick her out of university, and she'd be stuck working in a coffee shop for the rest of her life. Well, if this bloody pandemic ever ended and coffee shops could open properly again, instead of this takeaway bullshit where the café owners made minimal profit unless they pretty much worked for free, employed no staff and triple sanitised everything. She'd heard Tacey complain about the restrictions often enough.

Ooh, maybe Octavia, Tacey's sister, could help. She was doing a double degree with computer science, after all, and occasionally worked an IT helpdesk when she wasn't operating the espresso machine. If she stopped by the Shut Up Café on the way to uni, she might be able to catch Octavia and recover all her lost work.

It'd be so much easier if Jakob would only help her, like he used to do. Before he was internet famous, when they were both students together, he spent hours loading all the right software onto her laptop and setting it up for her. No problem was too big – he'd have done anything for her.

Whereas now…

"NO! NO! NO! You stupid fucking cunt! I told you to cast a spell, bitch, not kiss his arse! If you were real, I'd take all your armour off and spank you with your own sword until you bleed…"

Rochelle sighed. She knew he was actually shouting at his own scantily clad female avatar in the game, but sometimes, when he'd been gaming for several days straight, he got them mixed up and started shouting at her like that, too. It didn't help that she'd cosplayed his avatar at a convention last year, and he'd gotten so excited he'd actually tried to spank her.

She shuddered at the memory. She knew there were women out there who liked that sort of thing – or at least a whole lot of romance heroines who claimed to – but she'd happily lost the costume that very night and archaeologists would stumble across the Holy Grail before Jakob found that metal bikini again. Even if he did, there was no way she was wearing it again, and this time, the sword was definitely going up his arse before it went anywhere near hers.

See how the fans of his livestream liked watching that.

Jakob's screaming rant continued, so she headed outside, to do what she always did when life got too frustrating – she rid their yard of rocks. It didn't matter how many she picked up, there were always a hundred more waiting for her. Tiny limestone pebbles, some as small as her fingernail, and occasionally one as big as her fist. She wasn't sure if people threw them over her ageing limestone wall, or whether they fell off the wall of their own accord, sick of hanging in the air for more than a century.

Tonight, she filled her pockets with pebbles, then straddled the wall. From here, she could see right across Fremantle, all the way out to sea. Or across the art college oval to the buildings beyond, depending on which direction she faced. This time, she turned toward the school, or more accurately, the road that separated her back fence from the oval. The road was a sea of puddles, stretching right across the road.

If she angled it just right…

Rochelle skimmed a stone across the nearest puddle. It skidded through the water, sending up a small wave on either side, until it hit the kerb and stopped. Her second stone bounced up onto the footpath on the other side. The third one hit the low wall on the other side of the road, then bounced back into the puddle with a splash.

God, she couldn't even do this right. Maybe it was time to give up on all those dreams she'd held onto since high school.

Becoming an innovative filmmaker.

Splash.

Uploading short videos that went viral.

Splash.

Creating something that made people feel.

Splash.

Showing the world something they hadn't seen before.

Splash.

Walking the red carpet with her parents at her premiere.

Splash.

She didn't need a rock to shatter that particular dream – breast cancer had done it for her, when it grabbed Mum and didn't let go until she was a shadow of herself in the hospice.

She'd been in her first year of uni then, when she'd lost Mum, and that's when her bad luck had started. Mum had believed in her dreams, more than even Rochelle did, and without her…it was hard to find the enthusiasm for something when she was barely hanging on to a passing grade with her well-bitten fingernails.

She wished with all her might that someone

would help her, instead of shouting at her.

The last stone sailed right across the road, over the wall, and down onto the school oval, out of sight.

Oh God – what if she'd hit someone? It was late, and she couldn't see anyone playing sports on the oval right now, but what if some homeless person was sleeping in the shelter of the wall and been injured by her rock? She held her breath, listening, but no one appeared.

Rochelle sighed and let her remaining rocks drop to the garden bed. She should probably go to bed, instead of waxing miserable about losing Mum. No, she didn't need anyone else's help. She just need a good night's sleep so she could think straight, and sort things out for herself.

Maybe even some of her hope and determination would creep back in overnight. She'd need all her skills of persuasion to talk the lecturer into giving her an extension if Octavia couldn't save her.

EIGHT

Pain sliced into Ben's chest, and he let out a scream, flailing his arms until he hit flesh, and something went clattering away across the stone floor.

A man swore and stomped away.

Ben jumped to his feet, his head darting from side to side as he took in the room. His brothers lay where they'd fallen asleep, on the shelves, only now their chests were bare, with a bloodied circle on their left breast, over their hearts.

Or where their hearts should be, he realised as he took in the two bloody lumps on the table.

"Tor! Dunstan!" Neither man drew breath.

"You've killed them!" Ben shouted, lunging for the butcher.

But Pearse had retrieved the knife, which he now brandished between them with the sure grip of a man who knew how to wield a blade.

Until Ben kicked it out of his hand and followed it up with a fist to the man's face. He might not have his brothers' muscles, but he was the best fighter out of the three of them. And he was no honourable gentleman – convicts fought dirty, and Ben could hold his own with any of them. He soon had the butcher on his back on the floor, gasping for breath.

"Where did the gold come from?" Ben demanded, setting his foot on the man's throat.

"Williamstown…Nelson!" the man gurgled.

Not Fremantle, then. Likely stolen from its rightful owner, before being hidden here. So much for Ben's dream of taking a bag of it and fleeing with his brothers. Even if he were to kill the butcher and leave now, someone would still chase after him. He'd never be free.

But this man…this butcher…had killed his brothers. He deserved to hang for his crimes, even if it meant Ben spent the rest of his life in prison. He had to go to the guards, and bring them back here.

Ben scaled the ladder, shaking his head to clear it. Whatever the butcher had put in his tea was making him lightheaded. He climbed out into the cellar, only for the butcher to catch his foot, nearly upending him.

Ben kicked behind him, then kicked again until the butcher let go. But Ben didn't stop there. Another kick sent the man tumbling off the ladder to the ground, and he didn't get up again. Ben slammed the privy shut and staggered out of the shop and into the street.

"Help! Murder!" he cried, trying to run but he couldn't seem to catch his breath. Couldn't seem to stay on his feet. He felt himself falling, falling, and he was helpless to stop himself from smashing face first into the street.

He heard running feet. "It's a convict, fallen down dead drunk in the street. Fetch the guards!" someone said.

Yes. Yes. The guards would come and help. They'd listen to him. They always listened to him.

The stamp of boots heralded the guards. "Turn him over," one of them commanded, and rough hands rolled him until the back of his head hit the cobbles.

Ben struggled to speak, to open his eyes to see which guards had come, but he could scarcely move. What had been in that tea?

"Hey, is that blood? Bring the lantern closer."

A pause.

"It is blood. Looks like he's been stabbed. Better get him to the hospital, so they can patch him up."

"With a wound that deep, he won't make it to the hospital. Better take him up to the Skinner Street cemetery and bury him. He's dead already."

Rough hands hoisted him up, swinging him between them as Ben tried desperately to tell them he wasn't dead. But no words came out, and he couldn't feel his feet anymore. Or his legs. Or anything…

NINE

"Hey, Tacey, do you mind if I stick around for another hour or so, so I can redo the video footage I lost?" Rochelle asked.

"Octavia couldn't help you, then?" Tacey didn't look up from the massive coffee order she was assembling.

Rochelle shook her head, then realised Tacey wouldn't see it. "No. She says the files have completely vanished. But I figure I did so many takes, I could probably retake them all in about a couple of hours. It's the editing and the effects that will take the longest."

Tacey waved her hand. "Hey, if it's free advertising for my café, you can take as long as you like. As long as you make us look good."

Rochelle forced out a smile. "Well, that's the aim. I'll fail the assignment if I make you look bad. Advertising is meant to make you look good."

"Then by all means, film anything you like."

Rochelle started with some basic shots, closeups of Tacey using the espresso machine, steam rising off cups, and the food in the glass cabinets. Then there was a bit of a lull, so Tacey offered to make lattes for them both, taking her time turning the milk froth on top into works of art. Of course, the moment she was finished making them, a rush of customers came in, all exclaiming over how pretty they were, and asking for latte art of their own.

Rochelle carefully filmed each and every creation. She wasn't sure how to use them yet, but something told her she should. When she thought she had enough footage to work with, she sat down at one of the tables and downloaded everything. Then she started to edit, and add special effects, and…

She jerked out of her reverie as her computer emitted an alarming beeping sound as CRITICAL LOW BATTERY ERROR flashed across her screen. She fished about in her bag for the charging cable, but came up empty. She cursed as she hurried to save her work before the laptop shut down.

"Thanks, Tacey. I'll head home now, so I can finish this off and submit it. Who knows? If my lecturer likes it, maybe you can use it on some of the café's social media accounts."

Tacey laughed. "Yeah, thanks. This pandemic will probably be over by the time I get to updating our social media."

"Or business could pick up, and you can get us casuals to make the coffee again, so you can spend all of your days surfing the internet for your next hot date," Rochelle said.

Tacey shook her head. "Oh, no, I don't think I'll be dating again until Rory is. Or maybe not until she's finished high school, at least."

Rochelle couldn't remember the last time she and Jakob had gone out on an actual date, or even spent an evening together. Even before all the restaurants had closed for the pandemic, just going out for a movie or something. But that was different. They'd been together since high school, and were hardly in the first blush of love. They were living together. Only one step away from marriage and forever, really.

She sighed. Marrying Jakob didn't set her heart aflutter the way it used to. Maybe she was just too tired – working too hard to get this assignment done. Speaking of which…

"I'd better be going, so I can get this assignment in on time. Let me know if you need me to cover any shifts before then," Rochelle said, pushing the door open.

When she got home, she plugged in her laptop and went to grab a glass of water. The furious clatter of Jakob's keyboard told her he was gaming, and she knew better than to interrupt him in the middle of combat with some monster or other.

She opened the video file and set it to render, so she could upload it to submit it for assessment. When the rendering was done, she watched the final version, making sure she'd timed her transitions just right to match the music. Yep, it all came together perfectly – hell, now she wanted to go back to the café for coffee.

Maybe after she submitted the assignment, she could go get coffee with Jakob.

She tried to pull up the university website, but her laptop insisted the site wasn't available offline. Which made no sense, because she should be logged into the home wifi.

She checked her laptop settings, then told it to scan for the wifi, but it didn't come up. Oh, there were plenty of networks, from the houses and businesses around, as well as the school and the arts centre in the old asylum, but not theirs.

"Jakob?" she called, heading for the bedroom that was his gaming cave. "Jakob, there's something wrong with the wifi. Could you power cycle it, please?" God forbid she tell him to turn it off and on again, as if he didn't understand what power cycling was. He'd ranted for at least an hour last time she'd slipped up.

"No, the wifi's staying off. The only internet here is by direct cable to the modem, and I need all the bandwidth for my livestream. We're exploring a new area and I need it to run at the highest resolution, so everyone can see the graphics."

Rochelle sighed. "I just need it to submit an assignment. Five minutes, that's all."

"If it's only five minutes, you can wait until I'm done. This is important. This is live, Shellie, and my fans are counting on me to show them all the new content." He mashed the keys, then continued, "This is my livelihood here. Isn't putting food on the table worth more than some little project of yours?"

She couldn't remember the last time he'd bought food, prepared it, or even put something on the table she hadn't cooked. While she was this close to failing and being kicked out of uni for good. "If I fail one more assignment, they'll kick me out, Jakob. I need to submit it, or I'll be nothing but a university drop out."

"Dropping out? The connection can't drop out! We're almost through the minions and up to the big boss fight!" Jakob shrieked. "Oh my gawd, you scared the shit out of me. Now, go away and stop distracting me, Shellie. This is important." He actually made shooing motions, though his eyes stayed glued to the screen.

It was like she wasn't even there. She didn't matter to him, and even her degree and her life weren't as important as whatever imaginary monster he could see on the screen. He didn't care about her, or what she wanted, and as for marriage or partnership or some sort of forever…

Forever being ignored and screamed at? No thanks.

Rochelle wet her lips. "It's over," she whispered. The moment the words left her mouth, her heart felt lighter. "It's over, Jakob."

Of course, he heard that. His face turned red as his eyes focussed on her, fury flaring his nostrils. "It is not over. How can you say that? The fight is only just starting. Now, get out of here before I have to spank your ass in front of all my fans for distracting me from this very important boss fight. It's not funny, Shellie.

Can you see all the comments? They're flooding in. Every single one of my fans think you're being a brat. They want me to spank you. Now, get the hell out, or, so help me…"

His voice rose to a shriek, but she already wasn't listening. In fact, she'd marched right out of the house and into the yard, and she was perched on the back wall before his rant finally ended.

TEN

Dark. Couldn't breathe. So much weight on his chest…

Ben shoved at whatever it was with his hands, then got his shoulders under it and heaved, before he heaved again. Something was shifting…and there was sand…sand sliding down everywhere…like being buried alive…

No. He refused to die this way. He had to avenge his brothers' death. And Pamela's, too.

He had to live.

Ben clawed and fought, inching ever upwards, until he burst into the cold night air in a shower of sand and grass. He'd never loved the scent of limestone dust quite as much as he did now, even if he was coughing the stuff up on the damp grass.

He was alive. Alive and…

"Someone help me."

The words sounded in his head like the woman had whispered them right in his ear, but there was no one in sight.

But he had to help her. If she needed him…

"No, I don't need anyone's help."

Relief coursed through him, though he didn't understand why. Whoever she was, she was determined to help herself. He could respect that. If only Pamela had possessed such strength of resolve, maybe…

No. Whatever fine qualities Pamela had possessed had perished with her. There was no use wishing otherwise.

He needed to take stock of his surroundings, then make a plan. The guards would surely be searching for him. Unless they weren't, because they thought he was dead.

He turned, and saw what he hadn't before. He'd dug his way out of a grave. The guards had buried him alive. As far as they were concerned, he was dead. Which meant he was free to pursue whatever purpose he liked.

First, he needed to find out where he was. This fine lawn did not look like the cemetery, and he didn't recognise the building rising up along the edge of it, nor the limestone wall between him and the road. He scaled the wall and dropped down onto a road made of smooth black stone. Odd. What sort of…

Twin blinding lights appeared before him, the rumbling sound of swift wheels spinning on stone. But he couldn't hear the horses, nor could he understand how it could move so fast…

The driver couldn't see him, he realised just in time, leaping to the side and out of the carriage's path. He expected to collide with the limestone wall, but instead he sank into it, like the cold stone was little more than water. He barely had a moment to marvel at the sensation before he was out the other side, tumbling over and over on the dew-damp lawn.

Perhaps he should seek answers in the building first, then, he decided, picking himself up. And possibly some clothing, too, he added, glancing down at his naked self. The damn guards hadn't just buried him alive, they'd taken all his clothes, too. Well, not that they were his clothes, not truly, for they'd borne the stamp of the convict establishment, however small, but…Ben sighed.

He would investigate the building, find some clothing, and venture back to the butcher's house, for surely that was where answers were to be found.

The dark building beckoned, and as Ben strode across the lawn, a huge sign came into view, lit by lamps set in the ground. It was a College of the Arts, the sign said, and Ben laughed aloud.

Had he died after all and gone to heaven? For the one thing he'd dreamed about and wished for even more than coming to the Swan River Colony was that he might one day have the funds to be able to study art and learn to draw and paint like a true artist.

No, fate liked laughing at him, as she likely was now, for daring to believe he might have a place in heaven, after everything he'd done. This art college must be real, just as he was alive, though it seemed more miracle than sense.

But Ben would seize this miracle, and make it work for him, he swore, as he entered the hallowed portals of this mysterious art college.

ELEVEN

When the sun rose, Ben slipped between the walls of the college, as instinct told him he must, and it was not long before the corridors began to echo with footsteps. First, the confident strides of the tutors, which he was surprised to see were both men and women, though they dressed very much the same, as though the women tutors were required to dress like men. Then the students, uniformed in shades of blue, including a tartan skirt the length of a kilt, but worn by the girls.

This art college was wondrously strange. He could scarcely understand half the things they said at first, until he grew accustomed to their odd accents, and even then, many of the words were unfamiliar. Yet he drank it all in – every word, every picture that appeared as if by magic on the screen at the front of each classroom, or on the equally magical slates each student appeared to possess.

The classes were not just art, either – history and geography and mathematics and science the like of which he could scarcely believe. The lawn he'd been buried beneath was used for football matches, he found. Had the guards known they were burying him beneath a sports field? He hadn't heard a whisper in Fremantle of any kind of art college being built, but he could not deny the evidence of his senses. The school was as real as he was, and a veritable font of knowledge.

The miracle of its existence didn't truly dawn on him until he was eavesdropping on one of the history classes, of all things.

"Does anyone know when the gold rush began in Western Australia?" the teacher asked. She was one of the few women who wore clothing in a style Ben was familiar with — a shirt buttoned up to her throat and a skirt that swirled about her ankles as she walked.

Hands waved in the air, and the students began spouting numbers, which made no sense to Ben, or the teacher, either, who shook her head at all of them.

She tapped her fingers on her slate and a picture appeared on the screen at the front of the room.

"Gold was first found in Western Australia in 1885, at Halls Creek, then at Southern Cross, then Cue, before the big discoveries at Kalgoorlie and Coolgardie that necessitated the Goldfields Water Supply Scheme, a pipeline that travelled all the way to Kalgoorlie from Mundaring Weir, in the hills just outside Perth…"

She couldn't have said 1885. Yet there it was on the screen, along with a series of dates culminating in the finishing of the pipeline in 1903. History to this teacher and her students, which meant…

At the bottom of the screen, in tiny letters

and numbers he'd never paid much attention to, he saw the time, followed by the date. Today's date, if it could be believed.

Ben's breath caught in his throat. The day Pearse had butchered his brothers had been June 1855. The screen told him it was still June, but in the impossible year of 2020.

A hundred and sixty-five years had passed, while grass grew over his grave and an art school rose up beside him. No wonder fashions had changed, and the children's slates worked like magic. If he'd been born into this day and age instead of raised under the reign of Queen Victoria, would he have sat in this classroom, drinking in knowledge the like of which he could scarcely imagine?

Worse, he'd been right. There was gold to be found in Western Australia, and if he hadn't been imprisoned and then buried, he might have been the one to find it.

Fate must be laughing loudly right now.

Ben's thoughts spun. So much had changed in the century and a half he'd been buried. He couldn't even begin to imagine how he was alive right now. The butcher must have cast some sort of spell over him, which would not only explain his immortality, but the ability to walk through walls and the wings that appeared and disappeared at a thought. Not that he'd had much cause to use the wings, what with staying inside this school and all.

Why had Pearse awoken him? Why now? For if the butcher could turn Ben immortal, then surely he'd already performed the same spell on himself. Which meant Pearse was probably looking for him, and if Ben intended to seek vengeance for his brothers' deaths, then he needed to know as much as possible about life in this time, for Pearse was surely as comfortable here as he'd been in 1855 Fremantle.

So Ben haunted the school, a sort of corporeal ghost, soaking up all the knowledge he could, and observing the people of this time. The students reminded him of himself, during his school days – easily distracted, bored, not realising what a treasure knowledge could be. And the teachers… he kept getting distracted by the revelations each tutor seemed to be able to deliver in such a constant stream it left him breathless.

He felt wrung out, his brain about to burst out of his skull, when he went searching for something familiar.

He nearly cried when he stumbled across the art studio, a room full of students sketching with pencils, painting with palettes and brushes, and some even with pastels…Ben wanted to scream in triumph. This was the kind of art college he'd dreamed about, and here they taught art to children!

For a whole day, he feasted his eyes on all the art being created, until the children had departed and the sun began to set. Then, he surrendered to temptation, taking a box of pastels and a drawing pad for himself, before marching up to the hill behind the school to indulge in a bit of art of his own.

TWELVE

Staring out at the school oval, watching twilight descend, Rochelle's heart turned to lead in her chest. It was over between her and Jakob. Why hadn't she seen it sooner? He didn't care about her any more. He was already married to whatever game he was playing, and he didn't even see her past the scantily clad, sexy avatar he'd picked to fight for him.

Game over for them. It really was. She couldn't stop the tears now, streaking down her cheeks like teenage boys doing a dare on a late night Maccas run after the Year 12 ball. Okay, maybe her tears didn't look like cold shrunken teenage boy bits as they ran naked through the dining room, but they still made her shudder and wish she could close her eyes and unsee…everything.

If only.

She grabbed the top stone off the stockpile of rocks she kept up here and threw it as hard as she could. It flew clean across the road and bounced onto the oval below. One after the other, she hurled rocks, until they were all gone. Only then did she bury her face in her limestone-dusted hands, and sob a fresh flood of gritty tears.

Without Jakob, she had no one. Mum was gone, Dad was still up north, managing the cattle station, and who knew when she'd hear from him next, seeing as he was out of range of all but a satellite phone most of the time, and even that was only for use in emergencies. Ha. Her feeling lonely and miserable was hardly an emergency. She should be sad, or happy, or something, but right now, all she felt was angry.

Angry at herself for not noticing sooner. Angry at Jakob for being so selfish he hadn't even noticed her breaking up with him.

A snort of laughter escaped, breaking through her tears. Oh god, she was going mad now. Upset and angry and laughing all at the same time.

If anyone could see her…

And that's when she saw him. Across the road, at the lookout on top of the hill, staring right at her.

Rochelle wanted to shrink right down behind the wall and slink home.

But this was her house, and her wall, and she had every right to go mad here as much as anywhere else. Besides, staring was rude.

"What are you looking at?" she snapped.

He paused and cocked his head slightly. "Why, admiring the beautiful view, of course."

THIRTEEN

She stared at him as if she didn't believe him. Well, perhaps she couldn't see it as well as he could. "Come up here and take a look, if you like. It's well worth it," he said, beckoning.

The girl stiffened, her spine straightening out of that miserable slump as she drew in a deep breath. She was magnificent – from pitiful to empress in a single breath.

"You expect me to come up there?"

In truth, he didn't, though he would have liked it if she had. Then again, meeting strange men at night wasn't something good girls did — now or then, for some things hadn't changed. For all her delight in the picturesque, even Pamela would have hesitated. Not that it had saved her, in the end.

This girl, whoever she was, would not share Pamela's fate.

"Not if you don't wish to. Here, I shall come to you, so I can show you," Ben said, covering the ground between them in several eager strides.

She was the first person he'd spoken to since awakening in that grave. The first person who'd actually seen him. And if she could see him, then she deserved to see what he'd been drawing.

He held out his sketchbook, high above his head, for the wall she sat on was a foot higher than he was. For a moment, he thought she might jump off the wall and run away, until she looked down at the paper. And gasped.

"You've been drawing the sunset over the harbour. The cranes and the ships and the water, all dark shadows and reflections in a blaze of orange…it's beautiful," she breathed, taking the sketch from him to peer more closely at it.

"Well, the view is, or it was. The colour's fading now," he said, ducking his head. He wasn't sure he'd gotten the shade of the sky quite right, especially with the streaks of cloud across it. He was better with a brush, and watercolours or oils, than these chalky pastels, but the students had been learning to use them today, and his hands had itched to try them for himself. He couldn't imagine using pastels for a portrait yet, for he was nowhere near skilled enough for that, but a sweeping landscape…it was not his best work, but it was something, at least.

"I wish I could draw like this. Create a form of art that doesn't just vanish into the clouds every time my computer hiccups," she muttered, handing the book back.

He'd learned that the slates the school children used were sometimes called tablets or computers, and he'd seen them creating art on those, too, along with their other lessons. But what kind of art vanished into the clouds? Art that could fly?

He stopped to consider it. He'd learned of machines that could fly, so the thought of incorporating flight into art was…wondrous. Why, if he were to fly up to the clouds, he could draw pictures like what birds saw from up high. He wanted…nay, he needed to know more.

"Please, tell me more about your ephemeral art in the clouds," he implored.

She laughed. "When you put it like that, it almost sounds like when it disappears, it's part of what I intended, instead of just stupendous bad luck. Well, my preferred medium is film. Video, in all its forms, though mostly digital. I try to capture what's there with a lens, then after edits and effects and all sorts of things, make it into a movie that makes people feel something, or at least see something they didn't before. Even if it's for only a few seconds." She gestured toward his sketchbook. "It's not so much about skill in capturing the picture, or the footage, as being in the right place and the right time to see it in the first place."

Ben slowly nodded. He'd seen the students

doing something similar, capturing images of each other on their slates, or with the smaller devices they called phones. Sketching something would be so much easier if he could keep a clear image of it on a device, to refer to later. Something ephemeral, preserved forever. Or not forever, if it disappears.

"How does your art disappear, then?" he asked.

She frowned. "I wish I knew. I record it, I save it, and I back it up, and then when I go back to find it…it's gone, like I never saved it there in the first place. Sometimes I even get a heap of editing done, only for the files to vanish. Sometimes I don't even get to edit them. It's like I'm somehow deleting everything, every time I turn on my computer, but I know it's not me. I don't do anything to them. They're just gone."

"Maybe the clouds like your work so much, or they are jealous of your skills, so they steal it," Ben suggested. He'd known enough thieves in the prison, who'd had a thousand reasons for why they stole things. Envy was a powerful thing when others had so much more than you did.

She burst out laughing. "I'm only a student filmmaker, and barely passing my classes, so I can't imagine anyone being jealous of me. Unless it was an AI, because even I can do a better job than most AI..." She glanced behind her, at the house where Ben imagined she lived. "I should probably go inside and get some sleep, so I can get up early and submit my assignment on time. It was nice talking to you. Maybe if you're going to sketch the sunset again and you see me up on the wall, we could talk again? And you could show me more of your work?"

All his other work was long gone, likely lost along with his brothers. All he had was one hastily smudged pastel landscape, and she'd seen that.

But he could not disappoint a lady, so Ben mumbled something agreeable, before watching her slip off the wall and back into her house.

Once he was certain she was out of sight, he hurried back to the school. He had a lot of work to do, if he intended to show this girl what kind of art he could really create. For if she'd admired tonight's rough sketch, she could not help but be entranced by something more detailed. The sort of work that had earned him extra privileges in prison, or, before that, money to pay for their passage to the Swan River Colony.

It was only when he found pencils in the art classroom and began to sketch a fey maiden perched on a wall, that he realised he didn't even know her name.

FOURTEEN

Miracle of miracles, her video was still there the next morning, when she submitted it for assessment. But that didn't mean she could relax – she had one more assessment to submit for this unit, and it was the biggest of the lot. This assignment called for several short advertising videos of varying length, creating a story campaign. She'd been racking her brain all day to come up with something suitable for the Shut Up Café, which wasn't so cheesy it put people off.

It didn't help that she couldn't get that boy out of her head – the strange one who'd been sketching the sunset. She wished she'd gotten his name, or something, but the one thing that stuck in her mind was how intrigued he'd been by her ephemeral art.

Because…that's exactly what a social media video campaign was. It was ephemeral, meant to last only a short time, but it had to loom large in people's hearts, to move them, if only for a moment, so it stuck with them after the art itself was gone, or no longer in view. Like…a video that appeared in your social media feed. Or the picture on top of your coffee…

That was it!

All that latte art Tacey had created – did she still have the footage she'd taken? It had to be on her laptop somewhere…unless, of course, it had vanished into the cloud.

Twenty minutes later (half of them spent swearing), Jakob wandered into the kitchen and opened the fridge.

Rochelle took a deep breath. "Can you help me find some files that should be here on my cloud drive? I know I saved them…" It came out sounded more whiny than she wanted, but it seemed to work, all the same.

Jakob plucked the laptop from her hands and tapped away at it. "What files? There aren't any video files here."

She peered over his shoulder. She'd known the stuff she'd filmed in the café was gone, but now it looked like even the assignment she'd submitted had vanished, too. Good thing she'd already sent it this morning.

"They were all there yesterday…" she began.

He shrugged and set the laptop down. "You must have imagined them. There's nothing here."

"But they were here, and I can prove it. I was editing them last night. I submitted the final version this morning. The filenames still appear in the editing software, see? Only when I look in the folder, they're not there."

He was peering into the fridge again. "Where's dinner? Shouldn't you be cooking dinner instead of fooling around on your computer, looking for videos that aren't there?

I have a livestream starting soon, and you know I need to eat before my blood sugar gets too low, because you know what happens when my blood sugar gets too low."

He turned into a cranky, tantruming toddler, which was pretty much the case most of the time now.

Besides, she was already annoyed that he thought she was imagining things.

"I'm not fooling around on my computer. I'm doing my assignment, which I need to do to pass this unit, so I don't get kicked out of university, or lose this house, which I'm only allowed to stay in as long as I'm studying, in case you've forgotten. Besides, it's not my turn to cook. Tonight, it's your turn, because I usually do torchlight tours at the prison on Friday nights." Rochelle folded her arms across her chest. "Look, this really isn't working. When you moved in, we were both studying, and both doing half the chores. Well, except when you were helping me with tech support, and then sometimes I cooked while you dealt with the computing stuff. But if you can't even cook dinner when it's your turn, and you won't even let me submit my assignments when I need to so you can play games…"

"My gaming livestreams aren't just playing games. Between the ad revenue and the sponsorship deals, I'm the one bringing in the money here. Not you. If you don't cook dinner for me right now, you won't just lose the house. You'll lose me, too, and then you'll be the biggest loser there ever was. Now make me my dinner, bitch, and I want it on my desk before I have to go live!" Jakob flounced off to his den.

"I already told you it's over. I've already dumped your arse twice now, and you're too much of a loser to even listen, you lazy arse." She wrenched open the freezer. "You want dinner? Fine. Have one of the frozen meals you make when I'm working nights. I'll put it in the oven for you, but when the timer goes off, it's your problem." She peeled off the plastic seal, tossed the meal in the oven, and slammed the door.

Then she raced outside to climb the wall before Jakob saw her burst into tears.

FIFTEEN

More than anything, Ben wanted to sketch the town of Fremantle in daylight, from high in the sky, but he knew he could not step into the sunlight. How he knew that, he could not say, but there was such certainty in his body's instinct to hide from the sun, that he didn't bother to question it. His instincts were rarely wrong, and he ignored them at his peril…or worse, peril for those closest to him.

Not that he had anyone left to imperil, but…

A head appeared over the wall, before it was followed by a body. Ben's breath caught in his throat as she sat there again, legs folded beneath her like some sort of stricken elf, as she drew her arm back and pitched something clear across the road to the sports grounds below.

"I had hoped to see you again," Ben began, approaching slowly from the lookout, so as not to startle her. "Do you come out here every night?"

"No." Another missile sailed across the road. "Well, I never used to, but now it seems like maybe I do. It's funny, I'm not someone who needs or wants to be alone, but it's not so much wanting to avoid people as avoiding one person in particular. We've known each other forever. We even went to school together, and were best friends all the way through high school. We used to sneak over here to my grandmother's to hang out. Then she died and we became more and he moved in and now he just…isn't the same."

"You went to this art college?" Ben asked.

She managed a small smile. "Yeah, we did. I

stayed with Gran during the school term, then went home for the holidays. Well, until Mum died. I think that's what did it for Gran, really – when she lost Mum, she just sort of…gave up. I'd just turned eighteen, so Dad let me stay here on my own, as long as I was still at school, and then when I enrolled at university, he said I could stay until I graduated. Though I don't know if that'll ever happen."

Women who attended university. Graduated, just like men. Ben couldn't help but marvel at it.

"The university where you study film production," he said slowly.

She bobbed her head. "Yep. Though for how much longer, I don't know. I keep losing all the videos I film. I know I saved those coffee art videos. I'm certain of it. I…wait. I was at the café, and my battery was low. Maybe I didn't download them and they're still on the camera.. Then all I have to do is download them and I can get started on the assignment. Wow, just talking to you made everything so much better."

Ben ducked his head. "Happy to be of

service, though I don't believe I can claim much credit for you solving your own problem."

"Maybe not, but when I was upset about something back home, I'd go out to the yard, climb up on the fence and talk to the cows about it until I felt better, or worked things out. There were usually more cows than people, and I was never upset at the cows."

Ben laughed. "Sounds like where I grew up in Scotland. Only for us it was sheep. Can't say I ever tried to have a conversation with one, though. I don't remember them being very bright, or having much to say."

She laughed, too. "I couldn't imagine having sheep up there, though some of the station owners did, and then they complained about the dingoes. Dingoes and wild dogs could take down a sheep, but they were much more wary around cows, so we never had the same kind of stock losses. Most of them sold out, after too many bad years, but Dad's still up there, doing his thing, and presumably turning a profit. I honestly don't know if he expects me to take over one day, or if he means to sell the place when he wants to retire. I couldn't see myself running a station like that, though. I'd need a manager, if I could afford it. Or I could open it up to tourists as an artists retreat, maybe…"

"Artists who want to paint and film cows?" Ben enquired. He couldn't quite imagine it, but he'd heard of stranger things.

She just laughed. "Maybe. City people like to get a feel for the bush, and see a working cattle station, even just once in their lives. But the colours up there…the red dirt and the low scrub, the mountains just sticking up out of nowhere, ancient like they've been looking down on the station since the world began, wondering what these cows are doing on their land. So many birds, too – big ones, eagles and things. Oh, and the stars at night…it's almost like being up on the International Space Station, it's so clear. If you get a chance, you should see it."

Blood red soils, just like the stories had said. Maybe he should go and see it. Once he'd dealt with the butcher, of course.

"There are some working stations up near

Coral Bay and Exmouth that are geared for foreign tourists. Plus there are beaches and the snorkelling on Ningaloo Reef is unbelievable." She held her hands up, about a foot apart. "I once came this close to a shark bigger than I was. Luckily, it was a reef shark, so it wasn't interested in me. I think it was as surprised as I was, so it swam off, faster than I could follow it. Pity. I would've liked to get a picture."

A fearless lass who chased sharks in the water, in a world which allowed her to do such things. Ben shook his head. In all his wildest dreams, he could not have fathomed a future like this one. Or that he'd be here to see it.

A shrill beeping sound came from the house behind her.

She tilted her head, listening for a moment, before she said, "That's Jakob's dinner. Not my problem." She dropped down from the wall and held out her hand for his sketchbook. "What have you been drawing tonight?"

He'd been busy. This afternoon, he'd climbed to the highest point in the school, and stretched out beneath the roof, to try and sketch Fremantle in the afternoon light, as it was today. Clouds had rendered the ocean as grey as he remembered the waters of Scotland, so he'd stuck to a pencil sketch, turning it all into shades of grey. He'd wait for a sunny day before trying to reproduce the scene in watercolour.

But the beeping sound went on and on, and she grew increasingly uncomfortable, even as she leafed through his sketches.

"I'm sorry, I should probably go home and shut that off," she said, reluctantly handing back his book. Then she looked uncertainly up at the wall. "I didn't realise how high up it is on this side. Damn, I'll have to walk around, I think." She set off along the footpath into the darkness.

"Wait, I'll walk with you. To keep you safe," he said, hurrying to catch up.

"You don't need to," she said, but he could almost feel the relief rolling off her in waves.

So ladies walking alone were not safe now, any more than they had been in Ben's time. Sadness soured his mood. Maybe this future was not so perfect as it seemed.

"It's no trouble," he insisted, for he felt the

powerful pull to protect her.

If he'd been there to protect Pamela…

"What do you like to film, when you're not trying to catch sharks?" he asked, falling into step with her.

She gave him an odd look. "That was just the once, honestly. Underwater photography isn't easy, and everything moves so fast, it's hard to film anything. But even with the shark, it's…moments. I want to capture moments. Moments in time, so I can preserve them forever. Which probably means I should become a wedding photographer, or videographer, because that's all they do. But video, not photo, because I want to capture movement that just isn't there in a still shot. I mean, a photo is like one of those butterfly cabinets, with all the dead butterflies held in place by pins, or stuffed, taxidermised creatures with glass eyes. But a film…you can see the creature moving, it's like it's still alive. I mean, there's heaps of pictures of thylacines, Tasmanian tigers, and even a stuffed one at the museum, but someone recently colourised a video of one of the last living ones in captivity, and when you watch it, it's like it's alive again, instead of extinct for more than eighty years. Almost like resurrecting it from the dead." She took a deep breath, then let out a breathy laugh. "Listen to me dribble on about raising the dead. I know that's not possible, but…I'd like to film something that someone will look at in eighty years' time, so they'll feel like they've time travelled, if only for a moment."

Travelling into the known past, instead of an unknown future. If Ben could have chosen which way he'd have gone, he'd have chosen the past, so that he could change things. Save Pamela, and maybe his brothers, too. Yet here he was, in…

"This is me." She gestured at the front door of a cottage that looked like it had been here since Ben himself had arrived in Fremantle. A spacious cottage, by his standards, but so much smaller than the surrounding buildings. As if houses, much like the city itself, had grown over time.

She reached for the door handle, then her eyes widened in horror.

SIXTEEN

Rochelle reached for the door, only to realise the knob didn't turn. She'd left her keys inside, and now she was locked out. And if Jakob couldn't even hear the oven timer beeping its heart out, he definitely wouldn't hear her knocking on the door.

She'd have to dig out the spare key, in front of this friendly stranger she still didn't entirely trust…and find a new hiding spot when he was gone. And soon, before Jakob's dinner burned and set off the smoke alarm.

Rochelle took a deep breath, retrieved the key, and shoved it in the lock. As if by magic, the oven timer fell silent.

Dinner was definitely burned.

She wrenched the door open, onto have it yanked out of her hand and Jakob stood in the doorway, ready to explode.

Which, of course, he did.

"Where were you? Where have you been? Why did you let my dinner burn?" His nostrils flared, making him look more bovine than human as he scanned the street. When he caught sight of her companion, he curled his lip and roared, "Who's he? Were you cheating on me with this dickhead while my dinner was burning?"

He shoved past Rochelle to stand toe to toe with the artist whose name she still didn't know. "You think you can just come here and steal my girlfriend, noob?"

She grabbed his shoulder. "Jakob, don't. I told you, we're over, and I was just talking to him." Jakob was twice his size. One punch and he'd pulverise the poor guy, just for being nice.

Jakob shook her off. "Do you know who I am, noob? I'm Jakob Tollak, otherwise known as Iago, and I eat trash mobs like you for breakfast. Fuck off before I chew you up like toast."

The artist just grinned. He set down his sketchbook and actually took a fighting pose with his fists up and everything. "I never heard of you. Bring it, boy."

Jakob would crush him.

"No, don't…" Rochelle began, trying to step between them.

Only for something to collide with her head, sending her deep into darkness.

SEVENTEEN

The boy might be built like a privy, but he was clearly no boxer. Much like Ben had always been the smallest of all his brothers, but he'd easily been the best boxer. Quicker on his feet than Dunstan, quicker thinking than Torstan, with an artist's eye, he could see from the way a man's chest muscles moved as clearly as if the man had screamed it, long before he could land a blow. Which meant he knew where his fist needed to be, and where his body shouldn't be, in order to win.

The other convicts had thought him easy prey at first, but after he'd laid out a few of them in both fair and unfair fights, they'd soon learned to be wary of him, and his brothers.

This flapdoodle didn't stand a chance.

Ben easily dodged the man's first blow, and would have dodged the second, if she hadn't somehow entered the fray. Ben didn't think – he just reacted, putting himself within the foozler's reach to protect her. Only the fool jerked back in panic as Ben moved in, windmilling his arms to keep from falling over. One meaty fist collided with her cheek, and she went down, out cold from either his blow or the force of hitting the deck.

"Oh my God, you've killed her. This is your fault!" the flapdoodle screeched, pulling out his phone.

Before Ben could even deny such lies, the boy started speaking to someone on his phone.

If he hadn't seen the students at the art school doing this, he might have thought there was some sort of magic at work.

But right now, he didn't care about magic or science or whatever fuelled the boy's phone.

All Ben's attention was focussed on the girl lying at his feet. Breathing, thank God, but bleeding from a head wound somewhere under her hair. Ben was no doctor, and she definitely needed one. If he only knew where to find one, he'd be off at once.

"I need an ambulance, and the police, too. Some crazy guy knocked on our door and when my girlfriend answered it, he hit her! She's unconscious, and he's still hanging around." The boy aimed a kick at Ben. "I'm calling the police on you. Don't you touch her!"

The boy gave his name and the address, before he rounded on Ben again. "You did this!" he bleated. "You stay away from her, you hear, or you'll find out what they do to noobs like you in prison!"

Ben couldn't help it. He laughed. "Oh, I know all about prison. Why do you think I escaped? And it seems to me that you're the one who hit her, so you're the one who should get arrested, not me. All I did was walk the lady home."

The boy's eyes widened. "You

can't…you're…" He dropped the phone and bolted off down the street.

Ben considered going after him, to haul him back to face justice, but he couldn't leave her. He couldn't let the police catch him, either, but…he couldn't leave her. Even just the thought of deserting her horrified him. He had to protect her.

He didn't know how long he stood there, wishing he knew what to do, until the van pulled up, and two green clothed women got out, wheeling a narrow metal bed. The nurses or doctors or whatever they were moved with ruthless efficiency, checking her over before moving her onto the bed and wheeling her into the van.

Before Ben could decide whether to follow them or stay here to wait, a car with POLICE written in blue along the side pulled up where the van had been. Ben swallowed. It was too late to run now – they'd only pursue him.

And when they discovered he'd escaped from prison a hundred and sixty five years ago…Ben wasn't sure he wanted to know what they'd do.

If they recognised him. For he'd known all the prison guards, and he'd never seen these two before. Why, one was a woman, and the man was black. Yet both wore their uniforms with a confidence that told Ben there was no point challenging their authority – times had changed, and he needed desperately to adapt to them.

But he couldn't go searching for the butcher if he was back in prison.

An idea began to form. A mad one, but no madder than most of the others that had worked out well for him.

"What's your name?" the policeman asked.

Ben swallowed. "Jakob. Jakob Tollak."

The man just nodded and wrote it down. Like he believed him. "What happened?"

Ben decided to be a little braver. "She burned my dinner, so I got angry. I didn't mean to hit her, but she sort of got in the way, and she fell over and hit her head."

The policeman eyed him with suspicion, as well he might. "What about the attacker? Dispatch said there was another man?"

Ben swallowed again. "I made him up, so

help would come faster. She was unconscious, and I didn't know what to do. I didn't mean to hit her..."

The policewoman exchanged a glance with her colleague, and the man nodded. "If you'll just come with us down to the station, we can get this sorted out."

Ben closed his eyes for a moment. Back to prison, the last place he wanted to go. At least they didn't know his real name.

EIGHTEEN

"She's waking up. Miss, can you hear me? Can you tell me your name?"

Rochelle's head hurt and what was that beeping? Was it the oven timer or the smoke alarm? She just needed it to stop.

"Miss? Can you tell me your name?"

Rochelle squinted up at the woman in some sort of uniform. "I'm Rochelle Bourke."

"Do you remember what happened?"

She cast her mind back. The oven timer, worrying about the smoke alarm, Jakob fighting that kind stranger…then nothing. But if she had to guess… "I think…someone hit me?"

"Do you feel well enough to speak to the police about it? Because they've been waiting…"

She really didn't, but it was best to get this over with. "Sure." She struggled to sit up, and found her headache didn't throb quite as strongly when she wasn't staring right up at the bright lights.

A policewoman walked into the cubicle, then pulled the curtains back into place with a metallic scraping sound that set Rochelle's teeth on edge. She pulled a guest chair over so that she sat facing Rochelle and took out a tablet.

"Can you tell me your name and address, please?"

Rochelle sighed and gave her the details.

"My partner and I were called to your home earlier this evening, because of a triple zero call from a Mr Jakob Tollak, who also resides at your address. When we arrived, he was quite distressed, telling us he'd struck you and knocked you unconscious. He also mentioned something burning, but there were no signs of a fire. Can you tell us what happened?"

Accepting responsibility for his actions. How unlike Jakob. Then again, if he said he'd hit her, then he probably had. The one thing more unlikely than him taking responsibility for his own actions was him taking the blame for someone else.

"It was his turn to cook dinner, but he had work to do, so I put something in the oven for him and set the timer, then went for a walk. When I came home, I heard the timer beeping, and when I came in, he was shouting and gesticulating wildly. Then something hit me and I don't remember much else," Rochelle said.

"If your boyfriend hit you, then I would advise applying for a restraining order," the policewoman began.

Rochelle closed her eyes. "He's not my boyfriend. He was, but I broke up with him, or I tried to, and he won't leave."

"All the more reason to get a violence restraining order. He won't be allowed to come near you, so he won't be able to hurt you again."

Rochelle sighed. It didn't seem serious enough to need a restraining order, but…

"If he hit you once, he will do it again. The violence only escalates, until your life is in danger. The longer you stay, the less chance you'll get out alive."

If the police were able to scare him enough to make him tell them the truth, then he'd listen to them when they delivered the restraining order. "All right. Tell me what I need to do to make this happen."

NINETEEN

Ben expected to emerge from the police car at Fremantle Prison, amid the high limestone walls he and his brothers had hewn by hand, but instead, the policeman walked him into a brick building that sat between shops and eating houses, with only the POLICE sign out the front to signify it wasn't the same as its fellows.

And the cells…part cage, part ordinary wall, and they were empty. Ben breathed a sigh of relief. As soon as no one was looking, he'd be able to slip into one of the walls and be free.

He spent exactly sixteen minutes in his cell, according to the clock on the wall, before Ben made his escape. He waited for half an hour, to see if anyone would realise he was missing and try to give chase, before he decided no one actually cared what happened to him, and slipped through the walls to the street outside.

No one walking on the footpath seemed to notice him appearing in their midst — he was just another shadow in the night. On High Street, one of the signs told him. The same street the butcher's shop had been on, all those years ago.

For the first time since he'd awoken, Ben began to feel hope. Hope that he might actually succeed in finding the butcher and justice for his brothers.

TWENTY

Instead of going straight home from the hospital when they released her, Rochelle asked the taxi driver to stop at the Shut Up Café, where she could see Tacey serving customers.

"Hi Rochelle, what can I get you?" Tacey asked when Rochelle approached the counter.

Rochelle took a deep breath. "I need somewhere to stay."

Tacey's hand stopped wiping the counter mid-swipe. "Why?"

The story just sort of spilled out. Everything except the artist.

Until Rochelle finished up with, "So the police recommended I find somewhere to stay, until they have a chance to deliver a temporary restraining order to Jakob and he leaves my place."

Tacey winced. "I want to help you, I really do, but our place is packed to the rafters. I mean, there's me and Octavia and Rory, and with Sybil stuck in the Arctic, looking for ice mummies, we're storing her stuff, and Callie's housemates didn't make it in before the border closed, so she moved back in with us, in Sybil's room, when the lease ended."

"Seriously, I'd happily crash on a couch. It'll only be a week or two," Rochelle said, her heart sinking.

"I'd offer you the sofa bed if I could, but even that's not there any more. We had to store it upstairs here to make space for Sybil's stuff. Octavia sleeps on it sometimes when she's working on a film project in the studio she's set up upstairs…"

Rochelle dared to hope. "So you might have

space here?"

Tacey stared at her for a moment. "Actually, that's not a bad idea. There's been talk of relaxing restrictions, so we can have customers sitting at the tables inside soon, and I was hoping to open the café at night again. Octavia usually handled the evening shifts, but she's taken a fly-in-fly-out tech support role up north, so if you were willing to cover evenings at the café, I could let you stay here. There's no kitchen upstairs, so you'd have to use the café kitchen, but you'd have access to the upstairs staff bathroom, and of course the sofa bed…"

Rochelle clapped her hands. "Oh, that sounds perfect. I could use Octavia's studio to finish my media project, too."

"I don't know how busy the café will be in the evenings, or when we do reopen. We'll have to play it by ear, depending on how busy it gets. You might have to close early, or stay open later. If no one turns up, we might have to give up on evenings altogether until business picks up again, but you can still stay, even if we're closed. Well, until you get this thing with your ex sorted. Didn't you say the house where you were staying before was owned by family?"

Rochelle nodded. "It belonged to my grandmother. She put a condition in her will that I could stay in the house until I finished university. Whether that's because I graduate or get kicked out…who knows?"

"Of course you'll graduate. Without your ex around, making life difficult, I bet you'll do just fine. Will you need help bringing your stuff over? If you're willing to wait until I've closed the café and picked Rory up from school…"

Rochelle shook her head. Just the thought of subjecting a little girl like Rory to Jakob's mercurial moods or worse, more violence…no. Just…no. "I'll be fine. Most of my stuff fits in a suitcase, anyway, so I'll pick a time when Jakob is livestreaming, too busy to notice I'm there, pack what I need, and be back before you close in the afternoon. No worries."

For once, everything went as smooth as clockwork. Miracle of miracles, Jakob wasn't home, so it took less than an hour before

Rochelle was back at the café, unpacking her things in the surprisingly large studio apartment above the café.

"Use my equipment if you want to. I won't need any of it while I'm away, and I've just updated the graphics card on my computer. It's bound to be better than your laptop."

Rochelle jumped in surprise. "Octavia? I thought Tacey said you were up north!"

Octavia grinned. "I fly out again first thing tomorrow morning. Probably a good thing, too, so I can get you set up here. Oh, and I've been thinking about your cloud issue, with your files vanishing and all. Once or twice, I'd blame the software, but every single copy, everywhere you save it? No, that's malicious — either code or a person. I'd run a full system scan, and change your passwords. I bet that fixes it."

"I've never done either of those things," Rochelle admitted. "Jakob usually handles any of my tech support issues, and of course he has all my passwords."

Octavia shrugged. "Maybe he's been hacked, and doesn't know it. Anyway, first thing you do is change your passwords. Right now. And I'll set you up an account on my computer while you're at it."

Actually, she needed to change her passwords, anyway. All of them were pretty much on the same theme – Jake and Shelly 4 EVA – because when she and Jakob had set them up, she had thought they'd be together forever. What an idiot she'd been. She couldn't have been more wrong if she tried.

Tried and wrong…like Martha Rendell, the only woman they'd hanged at Fremantle Prison. A rushed trial with circumstantial evidence, for murder that might not have been murder at all, yet they'd hanged her anyway. Because people believed in evil stepmothers more than they believed doctors could make mistakes.

Well, Rochelle was done trusting the wrong people. She wasn't going to end up like poor Martha, and she'd set her new passwords accordingly, to remind her.

"You look like you're thinking real hard. Passwords aren't that difficult to create," Octavia teased.

Rochelle felt her cheeks heat with embarrassment. "Actually, I was thinking about Martha Rendell."

Octavia frowned. "Isn't that the murderess they say haunts the prison chapel? The one they hanged?"

Rochelle drew herself up, in full tour guide mode. "She was convicted of murder and hanged less than three weeks later, though she proclaimed her innocence up until the day she died. And she doesn't haunt the chapel. You can see her image in the chapel window from outside, on the parade ground, but you can't see her from inside at all."

Octavia grinned. "Ah, that put the spark back into you. Are you still running tours at the prison?"

Rochelle shook her head. "They're closed because of the restrictions. Hopefully, with everything opening up, they'll be allowed to run tours again, and I'll get to dress up and jump out at people."

Octavia shook her head. "I still can't believe you get paid to pretend to be a ghost. I mean the pay for doing IT support is good, but it's nowhere near as much fun as that."

"Well, I only get to be a ghost a couple of nights a week, and only when the prison's open for tours. While you're up north doing the superhero thing for people's computers, I'll be making a zillion coffees, and trying to turn each one into a work of art, like Tacey does. Have you seen the froth kitten she did on that cappuccino the other day? I'm sure I took a picture on my phone..." Rochelle fished out her phone and found the picture. "Here. There's a kitten...and a swan...and a heart..." As she flipped through the pictures, she found a video file. "Oh wow, here's the video I thought I'd lost. My battery was low, so I must have filmed it with my phone instead and forgotten. This is exactly what I needed for my assignment..."

Octavia touched two fingers to her forehead in a mock salute. "Well, don't let me keep you. You should be able to access everything on my computer just fine if you need to, and if you have any IT issues, feel free to email me. I might be stuck in a camp in the middle of the desert, but the internet access is better than the

CBD office here. I should know — it's my job to make sure it doesn't drop out."

Rochelle thanked her, and wished her a good flight as she plugged her phone into her laptop to download all the coffee pictures and footage. By the time she'd started the transfer, Octavia was already gone.

TWENTY-ONE

When the sun rose, Ben slipped inside the nearest wall to watch High Street in daylight. Great big digging machines ripped up the road, destroying what would have been days of back breaking labour by a convict work crew in a matter of minutes. There were no convicts present today – just men and women in eye-wateringly bright yellow and orange vests that dazzled in the sun.

By day's end, they had reduced the black-topped road to rubble, hauled away by a massive truck as the workers paused for their midday meal, and dug down into the sand to reveal pipes as thick as a man. Pipes that looked aged, yet they had not existed when Ben had walked this street. If he hadn't spent so much time in that art school, soaking up as much knowledge of this time as he could fit into his head, he was certain his brain would explode from the realisations he was forced to confront now.

The village of Fremantle he'd known had turned into a massive town, far grander than anything he could have imagined, which made finding the butcher an even more impossible task. Yet he would do it, if it took him a lifetime. He owed his brothers that much.

As the sun sank, the work crew went home, fencing their digging machine in a metal cage open to the sky, as different people emerged on the streets. People ambling along, eyeing off the eating houses as they passed. Shops closed, and people took up residence in doorways. Ben took them for beggars at first, until they began to spread their wares.

One man had a guitar, which he used to

great effect, singing along with his strumming to a tune Ben did not recognise, though many of the passersby appeared to, for they tossed coins into his guitar case.

A pair of women spread out cloth-covered boards that displayed a dizzying array of beaded jewellery in all colours of the rainbow.

But the stall that intrigued him most was where a man simply spread out a blanket, then laid sheets of paper across it like tiles. In the light of dusk, Ben could not see what was on the papers from across the street, so he emerged from his hiding place to take a closer look.

The pages were filled with pen and ink drawings, caricatures that captured a face or a likeness with only a few lines.

"Would you like me to draw you as a cartoon?" the man asked.

Ben blinked. He'd never known another artist with the skill to be able to draw him, yet it sounded like the most decadent thing to be drawn by someone else. "I don't have any money," he admitted.

The guy grinned. "Oh, that's all right. I'll

just add you to my gallery, then." He scrawled one line, then another, on the page before him, and held it up for Ben's perusal.

Ben gasped. He had not looked into a mirror since before he left Scotland, and yet here he was, immortalised in a few lines of ink. Dressed in the clothing he'd borrowed from the box marked LOST PROPERTY at the art college, he could have passed for one of the older students. No one would guess he should have been dead for more than a century.

"That's twenty bucks if you do decide to come back and buy it," the artist said, as he slotted the drawing into the pattern made by its fellows.

Ben nodded. He'd seen other people purchasing pictures from this man, so the price must be a reasonable one. "Do you make enough money to live off like this?" he asked.

The man shrugged. "Before the pandemic hit, I was making more than five hundred a night most Friday and Saturday nights. Double that if I set up in daytime near the markets, when there were tourists. Now, it pays the rent, but not much more than that. So I had to take a job up north, and now I only do this on my weeks off. Because I might just be a labourer at the mines, but I'm still an artist, and they can't take that away from me."

Ben couldn't help but agree. They'd taken his freedom and his family and his home, but as long as he'd had charcoal and paper, even in a prison cell, he'd still been an artist.

"If I do find a way to earn the money for it, are you here every night?" Ben asked.

The man shrugged. "Only on the weekends, and only when I'm not up north. I'm due to fly out tomorrow, so I won't be back for another three weeks."

Ben nodded. "See you in three weeks, then."

He forced himself to walk away, his mind whirling with ideas. Perhaps he might have a place in this city after all.

TWENTY-TWO

"It's not just coffee, it's art," Rochelle muttered to herself as she put the finishing touches on the ad campaign. Well, the ad campaign for her assignment, because she wasn't sure Tacey would want to use this to promote the café. It was cute and it was true, and the pictures of her coffee art creations were all kinds of wow, but the campaign just didn't seem…enough. It'd need one hell of a glow up to persuade her to really want to get a coffee here, and she loved Tacey's foam kittens.

Maybe she needed a sort of intro scene, introducing the café in one quick pan before zooming in on the coffee. Rochelle grabbed her phone and padded downstairs into the closed café. The only light came from the street outside, reflecting off metal and glass and casting weird shadows all around. Well, it could work for a Halloween ad, if she added some post production bats and things.

Rochelle laughed softly to herself as she panned around the room, then zoomed in on the espresso machine. The back of the machine reflected the street outside and what looked like Batman standing under the awning across the street.

Perfect for Halloween, even if it was still only June.

She edged closer to the window, trying to get a better angle on the dude in the costume. Actually, from this angle, he didn't look like Batman at all. Like some huge guy with wings and horns, not a guy in a suit.

Then a girl dashed into the shot, collided

with the guy in the costume, before they both just vanished.

Rochelle blinked, squinting at her phone screen before peering out the window. Yep, he was definitely gone.

They'd probably just gone inside the building. After all, he'd been standing in the doorway. He'd probably pushed open the door and slammed it closed behind them, while Rochelle had blinked. Because people could dress like superheroes or whatever, but none of those things were real.

It'd make an awesome ad for the café, though, if Batman or whoever he was got his coffee there.

Rochelle shook her head. She'd take a closer look in the morning, and see if there was anything she could do with the footage. Clean it up, maybe, because it'd be pretty grainy in the dark, and see if any of it was usable.

TWENTY-THREE

Rochelle shook her head. Whoever the guy had been cosplaying last night, it definitely hadn't been Batman. He'd had horns and wings for sure. She took a screenshot and ran an image search.

The first few hits were for some sort of hoax in the United States about a moth man. He had wings and antennae, not horns, but it was a pretty good match for what she'd seen. Only…Mothman comes to Shut Up Café for coffee didn't sound as exciting as Batman doing it. Even if you could see the café logo on the window in the corner of the shot…

Actually, the footage didn't clean up too badly. It was definitely clearer than some of the other blurry videos of the Mothman in other places in the world. Maybe she should post it online just for the hell of it…

Before she could second guess herself, Rochelle uploaded the video. For a caption, she called it: "Mothman comes to Fremantle High Street for coffee."

Then she went upstairs to get ready for work, because the restrictions were being lifted today. The café could allow people to sit inside at tables again, and Tacey wanted to open the place up at night, too. Rochelle had promised to make herself available all day and evening, in case she was needed, and it was looking like a lovely day outside.

After three months of restrictions, she'd want to be out in it, enjoying a coffee and whatever else she'd been missing.

She doubted even a Mothman sighting would stop most of the people of Fremantle from enjoying their newfound freedom.

And she wasn't wrong.

TWENTY-FOUR

When the cartoonist did not return the following night, Ben was there, ready to take his place. Armed with a selection of supplies he'd liberated from the art school, along with all the sketches he'd done since he awoke in this time, he had no trouble attracting the attention of passersby. In fact, he hadn't been in business for an hour before he'd delivered no less than three commissions, in a style he felt was far more complimentary than the cartoonist's caricatures.

When midnight came, and he was the lone person left on the street, he packed up his stall, pocketed his profits, and set off to search for what remained of the Fremantle he knew.

He followed High Street all the way to the hump of Arthur Head, still topped by the limestone Round House that predated the prison he and his brothers had built. Other structures from his time still lingered, sandwiched between more modern edifices of coloured stone and glass, and a bunch of brick buildings that spanned the time in between.

Th prison sat on its fortified hill, lording it over the town like a castle of old. It, too, had grown while Ben slept, sprouting new buildings and heightened walls, topped with sharp, spiked wire that would deter even the most determined climber.

But the butcher's shop was nowhere to be seen. Almost as though it had never existed, though Ben knew otherwise. He sighed. He knew the butcher would not be easy to find, but he'd hoped fate might smile on him for once. More than a century might have passed, but he was still the butt of fate's jokes.

Not for long, though. He was a free man, with money in his pocket and the means to make more, and if he knew anything about money, it was that the man who had it possessed infinitely more power than the man who did not.

As the nights passed, he purchased new clothes, more in keeping with the current fashions he observed on the men walking the streets of Fremantle today. When his pilfered art supplies ran low, he patronised a stationer's shop, for he had no need to steal them any more.

A signboard on the wall, covered in pieces of paper stuck to it with pins, caught his eye. There were advertisements for art exhibitions, and classes of all kinds. The one he could not look away from described a life drawing class, where students might sketch the naked human form. An evening class, too, which he might attend.

"Can anyone go to that?" Ben asked, pointing at the poster.

"Hmm?" The shop assistant turned to peer at it. "Oh, yeah, those art classes are up at the old asylum, the Fremantle Arts Centre. As long as you pay the fee, they're open to artists of all levels, from beginners to professionals."

Ben nodded. If he found and dealt with the butcher quickly, he'd be free to pursue his true passion, and attend art classes like this one.

Thanking the shop assistant, he scooped up his bag of purchases and headed back out into the night.

TWENTY-FIVE

Rochelle should have known. Less than twenty-four hours after she'd posted that Mothman video, the bloody thing went viral, so the first evening the café was open, it was chock full of conspiracy nutters, monster hunters and people who were probably just curious, eager for a glimpse of the mysterious Mothman.

The next morning, thrilled at the successful reopening, Tacey decided to offer a prize for anyone who could capture another picture of the Mothman. That brought them in in droves. Rochelle swore it was busier than she ever remembered it being before the pandemic. Between helping Tacey out during the day and manning the counter in the evenings, she barely had time to blink, let alone add anything to her assignment, so she submitted it as it was. She didn't trust the files not to vanish, though her cloud drive had been remarkably well behaved since she changed her passwords.

She considered warning Jakob that he might have been hacked, but the police had been adamant about avoiding him as much as possible until she got a court date for the restraining order. She should have heard by now, according to the police, but what with all the pandemic restrictions keeping the courts closed the last few months, there was a backlog of them to get through, so there was quite a wait. Which meant she'd be spending more time at the café, or in the apartment above it.

The lack of a kitchen was annoying at first, until she realised she wouldn't have time to cook anyway, what with working mealtimes.

Besides, there were usually leftover muffins and sandwiches at the end of the day, which meant she rarely had to cook at all.

When her assignment grades came through, Rochelle let out a whoop of triumph. She'd gotten credits for both of them, which meant she might actually pass this unit. Maybe she'd be able to attend university next semester, after all. Maybe even graduate.

She was so happy, she nearly danced all the way downstairs to the café, and her smile just wouldn't leave her face. Not even when two pushy, entitled customers wouldn't take no for an answer.

TWENTY-SIX

Ben had just set down his satchel, ready to unpack his wares for the evening, when he felt the inexplicable urge to be elsewhere right now. Actually, not so much elsewhere as across the road and closer to the water. He didn't think. He simply slung the satchel back over his shoulder and set off in the direction his heart tugged him towards.

He stopped outside a coffee house, its wide glass windows showing a brightly lit interior occupied by one woman and a pair of men who appeared to be standing over her in a threatening fashion.

Ben yanked open the door, gripping the handle so hard, the hinges creaked in protest.

One of the men glanced at him, frowned, then returned his attention to the girl behind the counter.

"Why won't you go out with me?" he demanded.

"In case you haven't noticed, I'm working," she said.

He couldn't see her face, but he'd know the elf maiden's voice anywhere.

"Just a kiss then," the man said. He sounded foxed.

"We don't sell those here. Just muffins, sandwiches and coffee. Oh, and cookies. Might I recommend the macadamia brittle afghans? Sweet and chocolate and chewy, perfect for keeping your mouth busy until your latte's cool enough to drink." Her smile hadn't faltered, though it did look forced. And there was fire in her eyes, like she was going to show them what one of her kind did to fools who displeased them.

More than anything, Ben wanted to pull up a chair and watch the fireworks unfold, but he was too much of a gentleman for that.

Unlike these two idiots.

"Here's your coffee." She shoved two takeaway cups toward the men.

"But we don't just want coffee. He wants you," the mouthy one's friend whined.

"Like I said, I'm working. Maybe you'll have better luck at one of the bars or night clubs up on the Terrace. Enjoy your evening." She turned away from them to meet Ben's eyes and a spark of recognition flared. "How may I help you, sir?"

The mouthy one glanced at Ben again, and his expression went from dismissive to mean. "Hey, we're not done with you yet."

A gentleman would have called these two idiots out to answer for their insults outside.

But Ben never had been, and never would be, a true gentleman. With two older brothers who were bigger than him, he'd learned to play dirty right along with the alphabet.

He grinned. "Yeah, you are. You've got what you ordered. Now go."

Mouthy's mate looked him over. "Beat it, runt. Get back to Timezone where the other kids hang out."

"But this is where they make the best coffee. And the best cookies." Ben smiled. He didn't care if the coffee tasted like tar, but he did like the sound of the cookies. "I'm hoping she'll be done with me before the police patrol get here, because it looks like they're ordering for the whole precinct and that'll take forever. Luckily, they stopped to deal with someone who was drunk and disorderly, or they'd have beaten me here."

Ben counted to five under his breath before the door slammed behind both of them.

She squinted at him. "You're making a habit of this. Showing up when my bad luck's taking a turn for the worse. Are you some sort of superhero or something?"

Superheroes. They were characters in the comic books some of the school students had.

Ben shook his head. "Sorry. I'm no comic book hero. Just a man in search of good coffee and…did you say macadamia brittle cookies?"

She laughed. "Actually, those cookies are

stale and not supposed to be sold. But I kind of like them chewy, when they're three days old. And they go really well with frothy milk, which is basically what those guys had ordered – topped up lattes with only half a shot of espresso. Oh, and when they're chewy, they tend to stick your teeth together, which I figured might shut them up for a minute..." She ducked her head. "I'm sorry, I'm normally really nice, and I've been in a good mood all day, but guys like that just bring out the worst in me. All the maturity of a three year old, convinced the world exists only to pander to their whims."

"Like...ah, what was his name? Jakob Tollak?"

Her expression darkened. "Yes, exactly like him. But he's not part of my life any more, because all I seem to do now is live and breathe coffee, or the occasional tea or hot chocolate. Speaking of which, what can I get you? Oh, and I promise if you order a latte, I'll do proper art on top, and not a dick."

He blinked. Did she really just say...?

She closed her eyes. "You don't believe me.

I know, I know, it's childish, and I shouldn't have, but…" She unclipped her phone from the little tripod it had been standing on and swiped her finger across the screen. "Here. I've been filming all the art for an ad campaign."

Sure enough, she'd poured the milk in a pattern that looked exactly like an erect cock and balls, with a dusting of hair and everything.

Ben couldn't help but laugh. "That's very…" He wasn't sure if he should say accurate, or anatomically correct. She'd obviously seen the real thing, to be able to represent it so accurately, but…

"Juvenile?" she supplied. "I know. I probably should've just stencilled a moth on it in chocolate powder, like I've been doing for everyone else tonight. Like I'll have to do if half the police precinct are coming in, seeing as we close in less than half an hour. Are they really headed here?"

Ben shook his head. "I'm afraid I lied about the patrol. I haven't seen any police officers tonight." Which was a good thing, given he'd escaped his prison cell the other night. "But I would like a black coffee, please. Just black. I'll provide my own art." He tugged his sketchbook out of his satchel.

She smiled. "One espresso, coming up." She concentrated on the coffee machine, which hissed and steamed like some sort of angry dragon. "This is how I drank my morning coffee in Italy. Now, the art I saw there…just everywhere…centuries of creating the most amazing things and preserving it so it's still there…" She shook her head. "Have you ever been to Italy?"

Ben shook his head. "I've always wanted to go. One day, maybe…"

She slammed both hands on the counter. "You need to. Every artist needs to. The Sistine Chapel alone is worth the trip. I mean, you're only supposed to stay there for fifteen minutes, but I managed to get in just before a tour group, so I got twice that, but I could have just lain on the floor, looking up at that ceiling all day."

"Would you come with me?" The words had left his lips before he'd thought them through, and all he could do was curse his stupid tongue, for sounding as bad as the idiots who'd just left.

But she wasn't looking at him the way she'd regarded them. No, she was thoughtful now.

"You know what? When the borders open, if I can scrape up enough money for the plane ticket…yeah, I would absolutely love to visit the Sistine Chapel with you. It'd be interesting to hear what you think, a talented artist seeing it for the first time."

"It's a date, then."

Modern words coming out of his mouth – he couldn't say where he'd heard them, but they seemed right, somehow. He stared at her, and she stared right back.

After a long moment that stretched forever, she shook her head, and broke the trance. She brought out a small cup of coffee and snapped a lid onto it. "There you go."

Ben stared at the tiny cup. "Do you mind if I drink it inside the café, instead of taking it away with me? I'll sit over by the window, where I won't disturb you, so I can draw."

"Sure. I…I should have asked if you wanted it here, or to take away. I was just so flustered by the previous customers, I didn't think…oh, and you wanted a cookie, too, didn't you? The choc chip are the best. Tacey made those fresh this morning, and I swear, there's about as much chocolate as cookie in them. I don't know how she does it." She reached for the jar.

Ben lifted up his hand to stop her. "Don't worry about it. The coffee is fine. I'll come back and have a cookie next time."

"If you're sure…"

He nodded mechanically, and moved toward the table, though every step away from her felt like he was wearing manacles, they were so heavy.

Other customers came and went. In between, she cleaned the café, wiping a cloth over each of the tables, before stacking the chairs on top of it. Then she flipped a sign on the door and headed for the coffee machine. Whatever she did to it made it steam and smoke and shriek, but the dogged determination in her expression told him she would complete her task, whatever it was, before she finished work for the night.

His sketchbook and pencil were in his hands

before he'd even really thought about it, trying to capture the elf maiden subduing her mechanical dragon.

When she left to carry some dishes into the kitchen out the back, he made his escape, tipping his coffee into a nearby pot plant before slipping out the door to the street outside.

But something made him tear the picture out of his book, and leave it behind for her. It belonged to her more than it did to him, capturing a private moment of victory that no one else but them knew about.

Much later that night, when dawn's light touched the eastern horizon, he slipped inside the walls of the café, curious to find out what she thought of his gift, or if she'd even seen it at all.

The table had chairs on top of it now, with no sign of his picture, so she must have liked it enough to take it with her.

Satisfied, Ben headed for the roof, where he had only moments to take wing and fly to the school, before sunrise confined him to the shadows again.

TWENTY-SEVEN

"So, how are the evenings going?" Tacey asked. "I mean, I can see from the figures that we've had a nice uptick in sales since the restrictions lifted, or maybe it was just because of your viral Mothman video, but that seems to have died down now, so…how are the evenings going?"

"Really well. Almost like we'd never had any restrictions. Business as usual, only…busier." She ducked her head, staring at the froth kitten on the side of her cup. Even the kitten's soulful eyes seemed to want to beg her to 'fess up. "Of course, we still get our share of entitled arseholes, and more of them now the pubs are open."

"What happened? Do we need more security?" Tacey asked instantly.

And that was why Rochelle loved working for Tacey. She actually cared that her employees were safe, instead of dismissing their concerns. Then again, Tacey knew what it was like not to feel safe…

Rochelle shook her head. "It was just a couple of drunk idiots who caused trouble because I was here alone. The moment another customer walked in, they backed right off and left."

"But what if that customer hadn't walked in?" Tacey asked, echoing Rochelle's thoughts.

"I honestly don't know, but it's not something I've had to worry about since, because he's been watching." Rochelle pointed out the window, to where the artist was setting up his stall in front of the stationery shop across the road. "The customer who walked in has a stall on the footpath most nights, drawing portraits of people. He said if I ever have any trouble, or need his help, just wave and he'll come right over."

"Do you know him?"

Rochelle hesitated. "A little. He lives nearby. The night Jakob…he was there that night. He tried to help, and Jakob got angry at him instead of me."

Tacey nodded slowly. "So because of him, you weren't injured worse."

Rochelle wanted to nod, but she'd been unconscious. She still didn't know what had happened between getting knocked out and waking up in hospital, but the police had been there, and they'd advised her to get a restraining order, so…

Tacey seemed to be able to read the answer from her expression, even without words. She dusted her hands on her apron. "Well, I guess I'd better go out there and talk to him." Without another word, she marched out the door and across the road before Rochelle could stop her.

Of course, then some customers came in, so Rochelle couldn't even watch the exchange, as she had to concentrate on getting their coffee order right without burning herself.

When they finally left, and Rochelle had a chance to glance out the window again, both Tacey and the artist had gone. She sighed in frustration.

"You got a sec, Rochelle?"

She blinked. Tacey was sitting at a table in the corner with…

"Rochelle, I'd like to introduce you to Ben Stone. As of next week, he's going to be our artist in residence in the evenings, and this table will be reserved for him and his clients. Give him staff rates for anything he wants, same as the rest of us." Tacey hitched her bag higher on her shoulder. "See you tomorrow." And she left.

Leaving Ben Stone standing there with a big grin on his face, and his hand out for her to shake.

Rochelle mentally shook herself for spacing out. She couldn't be mesmerised by his smile. It's not like this was their first meeting. She knew he was Scottish and he'd never talked to cows or sheep. And he could draw the most beautiful pictures…

She took his hand. Warm and firm beneath her fingers, yet he didn't try to crush her hand like some guys did. He held her like he was afraid he'd hurt her.

"Ben Stone," he said. Of course with a smile.

"Rochelle Bourke," she replied. "I never did get to thank you properly for what you did the other night, or for the picture."

His grin only widened. "Did you like it?"

She swallowed. "Did you have to make them look like penises? I mean, you made me look good, but I imagine if they'd really looked like dicks, I wouldn't have been able to look so serene, handing two cups of coffee to two giant, walking penises!"

He sighed. "So you didn't like it. Then I shall endeavour to draw a portrait of you that you do like, on my first night as an artist in residence next week."

Rochelle felt her cheeks redden. "I didn't say that." Actually, she'd pinned the picture up on the wall upstairs, until she'd worried that Tacey's young daughter Rory might see it, and then she'd reluctantly taken it down. "I just…well, I can't exactly put it on the wall or show it to anyone, can I?"

Ben laughed. "No, I imagine not. My promise still stands – I shall draw you a new portrait, one suitable to hang on the wall and show everyone. In colour, not just a quick pencil sketch. In between my real task, which is to be your protector."

That last line touched a deep chord in her, a sort of unknown harmony she couldn't explain. It felt…right, while at the same time… "You don't have to do that. Honestly, I think all Tacey wants you to do is be a presence in the café, not to actually…well, not like that night Jakob tried to fight you. That's just…"

"I think I owe you an apology for that night. If I had not walked you home, he would not have challenged me to a fight, and you would not have been injured." Ben bowed his head. "So any injuries you suffered that night were my fault."

Rochelle stared at him. "You mean…you hit me, and not Jakob?" And now she was alone with him. Oh God, she had to get him out of here. Or she had to get out of here.

"Of course not. I would never hurt a woman. His blow was aimed at me, but then he panicked and hit you instead. The hand that struck you was not mine, but I am still to blame."

Rochelle relaxed. Okay. He could stay, then. "No, don't apologise for him. He blames other people enough as it is. It was the last straw, and I'm better off without him. In fact, I'd like to forget he ever existed."

Ben bowed his head. "On this, we agree. It shall be as you wish. I shall never mention his name again."

And she believed him.

TWENTY-EIGHT

Of course, the next morning threw a spanner into the works – right in the middle of her email inbox. Fremantle Prison was starting to do tours again, and they wanted to her to resume her role as one of the night tour guides. So much for spending every evening with Ben at the café.

Rochelle considered saying no, that the café was now giving her enough hours for her to give up her second job, but…

She liked doing the tours. For a couple of nights a week, she'd dress up in costume and pretend to be one of the prisoners, jumping out at visitors and telling her sorry tale. Martha Rendell couldn't tell her own story, so someone else had to do it for her. And while most of the tour guides had their facts straight and didn't sensationalise the tale, occasionally one of the actors on the night tour would make her out to be the evil stepmother, a villain who'd surely deserved her fate.

No. She wanted her job at the prison more than she wanted to make coffee for Tacey. And she'd need both jobs when she got her house back, because she'd have bills to pay, and she'd be paying those by herself, instead of splitting them with Jakob. Not that Jakob had ever remembered to pay his share of stuff…

A quick chat with Tacey sorted things out. Keeping the café open in the evenings was definitely profitable, so Tacey would call in one of the casual staff to cover any evening shifts Rochelle or Octavia couldn't work. Rochelle could work her shifts at the prison and at the café, no worries.

Except…that was two nights she wouldn't see Ben.

Rochelle nearly laughed at herself. She barely knew the guy, and now she was pining for him when they were apart? Since when had she turned into a clingy teenager again?

She'd see the man five nights a week, which was more often than she saw most people. Even Jakob hadn't come over on weekends when she'd lived with Gran, because he'd had family things to do on the weekend.

Ugh. Enough about Jakob. She was trying to forget he existed, at least until the court hearing, which couldn't come soon enough.

TWENTY-NINE

The first few nights Ben came in, she barely got to speak to him. She was kept so busy serving customers, she didn't get to leave the counter, and while her eyes kept darting to the corner where he had his own steady stream of clients, he never came up to her, not even to order a coffee.

Before she knew it, it was closing time, and when she crossed the café to turn the sign to say so, he'd uttered, "Good night, Miss Bourke," and departed. Every night it was the same, until she was so frustrated she wanted to scream. Just five minutes. If she could speak to him for just five minutes…

Almost as if he was taunting her, he left a new picture of her on the table every night. She checked them over, making sure he hadn't included any dicks or other not safe for work bits, before adding them to the growing gallery on the café wall, beside the sign that said he took commissions. In the absence of commissions, he'd taken to drawing the café staff and patrons. He'd already captured likenesses of most of the café regulars, in a combination of pencil sketch and watercolours.

Rochelle's favourite was one of a kid who came in with her dad for a hot chocolate once a week, a treat Rochelle believed was a bribe for attending some sort of appointment the girl didn't enjoy. Tacey usually gave the girl a froth kitten or puppy in her cup, but Tacey had gone home, so Rochelle had been forced to try her hand at froth animals. The result came out more like a teddy bear than anything she'd seen Tacey create, but the girl's eyes had lit up when she saw it, and Rochelle had felt a momentary warm glow inside that she'd succeeded.

Ben had captured the light in the girl's eyes as she stared at the bear, the moment so real Rochelle wanted to reach out and touch it, even though it was really just a piece of paper stuck to the wall.

She wanted to draw people in with her films, to make them feel, but Ben did that effortlessly, with a stroke of his pencil and a flick of his brush. She was dying to ask him how he did it. How he breathed such life into a simple piece of paper, and whether he could teach her to do the same.

But she couldn't ask him if she never got the chance to speak to him.

Shaking her head, Rochelle stacked the chairs on his table, and began sweeping the floor. When she knelt down to scoop up the day's mess in her dustpan, she caught a glimpse of movement on the building across the road.

She pressed her face to the window, peering out into the darkness. Or where the darkness seemed to grow darker, as it started to dance…

She abandoned the dustpan and dashed upstairs, her phone in her hand before she could remember pulling it out of her pocket. From the upstairs window, she had a much better view.

The dark shadow she'd seen from below was clearer up here, and she thumbed the RECORD button on her phone so she didn't miss a moment of the performance, for that was definitely the word for it.

The Mothman had returned, and he had some serious moves. Only this time, he wasn't on the footpath, but on the rooftop across the road. She wished she could hear the music he was dancing to, but she'd have to open the window for that, and then he'd surely spot her and stop.

So she watched, transfixed, her eyes darting from her phone to the scene before her, not quite believing her own eyes.

Because even with Tacey's offer of a month's worth of free coffee, no one had managed to capture a second picture of the Mothman. Like he'd been hiding until now, and he only came out when she could see him.

Or maybe he came out every night, but she'd usually gone to bed, so she didn't see him, more like. Because he might be shaking that peach-shaped butt just for her, or maybe this was all for someone sitting on the roof, where she couldn't see. She knew there were apartments across the road — one of the women who lived there had a thing for Tacey's muffins, and she bought more muffins than coffee. Rochelle had scribbled her name on a coffee cup a few days ago, though…what was it? Something starting with A…Annelise? No, it had reminded Rochelle of snorkelling and the sea…Anemone, that was it!

Next time she saw her, she should ask Anemone if she'd seen the Mothman. Maybe even mention the free coffee, to see if she got a response from the woman. Because if she had a man who could dance like that, costumed or not, Rochelle would want to keep him a secret, too.

Oh God, he'd seen her. The man with the wings winked at her, then turned around and shook his butt at her, before jumping down out of sight.

Rochelle whirled around, putting her back to the wall beside the window, and stopped the recording with a swipe of her shaking finger. She half expected him to fly over here like Batman and demand her phone and the footage.

Then she laughed at herself for believing the man in the suit could actually fly. Oh, his wings had looked real enough, but they wouldn't support his weight. They were a costume, not part of him.

She focussed on her phone screen, and played back the video. Yeah, it was dark, but there was light enough to see the dude dancing on the roof. If she used some of Octavia's video editing software, she might be able to clean it up enough to upload it and have a second viral video bringing droves to the café.

A project for the weekend, then, she decided, as she stuck her phone on the charger.

After she'd finished cleaning and closing up the café for the night.

It wasn't until she was lying in bed that

night that she wondered what Ben would have made of it, watching that dancing winged man across the way. How would he have drawn him?

Ha, Ben probably would have captured the wink and the butt wiggle, the moment she'd known he was staring right at her. That moment when her heart had stopped, then beat double time, as she'd been torn between panic and the need to watch whatever was going on. Wanting to run away, yet also wanting to step closer.

Yep, she'd definitely been bitten by the crazy camerawoman bug. The one that made her want to capture a moment, instead of running away like a sensible person.

Rochelle sighed. She'd done sensible. Maybe it was time for a little more crazy in her life.

THIRTY

A girl Ben didn't recognise stood behind the café counter. "Where's Rochelle?" he asked, dropping his satchel on his usual table.

"She's not working tonight," the girl said primly.

Tacey breezed out of the kitchen, carrying a steaming tray of clean cups, fresh out of the dishwasher. "Oh, hi, Ben. This is Crystal. She'll be covering Rochelle's shifts while she's at the prison."

Ben's heart stopped. "Why is Rochelle in

prison?"

Tacey laughed. "She works as a tour guide at the prison. Dressing up in costume and pretending to be one of the prisoners for tourists. There aren't any real inmates any more – the place is for tourists now."

"Oh." Ben felt like a fool. Then again, in how could he possibly have imagined the prison he and his brothers had escaped before it could sap the life from them was a place people chose to visit for fun? The future was a very strange place.

"She might be back before the café closes. She said she wasn't sure how late the tours would go, seeing as they'd only just started up again."

Ben nodded. He could wait.

The hours passed quickly, as word had evidently spread, and a gaggle of girls all wanted their portraits drawn before they went dancing. Before Ben knew it, Crystal was flipping the sign on the door to CLOSED.

Ben threw his things back into his bag. "Good night," he called over his shoulder as he hurried out the door. It was a short walk to the prison, but he made the trip shorter still by climbing onto the roof and flying there instead. He dropped down in the shadows of the outer wall, then made his way to the gatehouse.

It was strange to see the gates wide open, and brightly lit with electric lighting. Despite the white limestone walls, he'd remembered this as a dark place. Not the sort of place Rochelle belonged at all.

Nor the kind of place where there should be a gift shop, yet that's where he headed, for the signs said to ask there about tours.

The woman behind the counter was busy selling miniature manacles and whips to a group of middle-aged women who giggled as they pretended to flog each other. These women had likely never been forced to stand witness to the real thing, watching the blood splatter as grown men groaned and cried in agony.

Ben shook his head. Best not to think about the time they'd whipped Torstan within these very walls, for daring to tell the truth about how shoddy the work on the walls was. If Torstan could only see that the walls still stood, he would shake his head in wonder. But Torstan would never see these walls, or anything else again. He'd died trying to escape them, and in the end, he had. He was resting in peace now, had been for more than a century, and his blood had surely been washed away while Ben slept.

"Can I help you?"

Ben stepped up to the counter, summoning a smile. "Hi, I was wondering if Rochelle's finished yet. We were expecting her home earlier."

"I'll check," the woman said, picking up what looked like a chunky phone that emitted a hissing noise. "Nine fifteen tour group, have you made it to New Division yet?"

Garbled words came out of the device too quickly for Ben to comprehend, but the woman just nodded sagely, said, "Thank you, over," and put the phone down. Then she turned back to Ben. "She'll probably be another half hour, at least. If it weren't so late, I'd say go get a coffee from the café outside while you wait. Maybe just take a seat at one of the tables instead. I can sell you a book to read about the history of the prison, if you like, but if you're a friend of Rochelle's, you probably know all about the history of this place, and the prisoners who lived here."

Ben forced himself to return her smile. "Yes, I do." It came out bleaker than he intended, but she didn't seem to notice. Or perhaps she mistook his tone for something more light hearted.

"I'll tell her you're waiting when she's done," the woman said, dismissing Ben with her eyes as she turned to help another customer purchase a doll in arrow patterned pyjamas that looked nothing like the convict clothing Ben and his brothers had worn.

Shaking his head at the insanity of it all, Ben found the closed coffee shop and ensconced himself at one of the outside tables with his sketchbook.

THIRTY-ONE

Rochelle liked acting, but she definitely didn't like doing it in Victorian women's clothes. Some parts of the past definitely belonged in the past, she told herself as she shucked off the swishy skirts and eased back into her jeans. But it was worth it if it made the couple hundred people who'd toured the prison tonight question what they'd heard about the prison's inmates, and whether they were as guilty as they'd been painted. Maybe if enough people believed in her innocence, Martha Rendell's ghost might finally be laid to rest.

"What a turnout," Karen said as Rochelle walked out of the costume cupboard. "We had to put on four extra tours and push some of them into next week. How did it go out there?"

Rochelle smiled. "Very busy, and I admit I'm a bit rusty, but after the first few, I got my timing right, so I could pop out and spook them. I think I got my first scream on the seven thirty tour, or maybe it was the seven fifteen. It's good to be back. See you on Wednesday, if you're working then." She waved and headed out.

"Oh, your friend's waiting for you outside the café. He said he was worried you hadn't come home yet."

Rochelle froze. Jakob. It had to be. "Is there another way out I can use to avoid him? I'm…I've filed for a restraining order against my ex, but the courts are being slow, and I don't want to run into him."

Karen clapped a hand to her mouth. "Oh, I'm so sorry. He was so nice, I didn't think he could be anything but your friend. He's been sitting at one of the café tables drawing for over an hour now."

Rochelle dared to breathe again. Jakob could barely draw stick figures, and he hated any art that wasn't in game. She risked a peek out the window and nearly laughed.

Ben sat cross-legged on one of the benches, peering up at the gatehouse as the pencil in his hand seemed to move almost of its own accord across the page.

"Shall I tell him to leave because we're closed?" Karen asked, wringing her hands.

Rochelle shook her head. "That's my friend Ben, not my ex at all. He might draw a mean cartoon with that pencil of his, but he's no John Wick. Definitely harmless." She headed out into the courtyard to greet him.

"What are you doing here?" she asked.

Ben pointed at the gatehouse clock. "I've been drawing the owl. She's hunting the moths flocking to the light up there. Here, take a look." He held out his sketchbook.

Sure enough, he'd drawn a dozen different vignettes of what appeared to be a small boobook owl, swooping out of the darkness to catch moths, before disappearing again.

"Here it comes again," Ben said, pointing.

Silent as the night breeze, the owl drifted over the gatehouse. Suddenly, the creature darted upward, its talon snatching a fat moth out of the air, before the owl vanished over the wall.

"Wow," Rochelle breathed. "I've worked here so many nights, and that's the first time I've ever seen an owl at the prison." Her shoulders slumped. "I should have gotten my phone out and filmed it."

Ben shrugged. "We could wait and see if it comes back, if you like."

"No, they're closing up. We have to go. But we could come back another night, or I could." He still hadn't answered her question. "What are you doing here?" He couldn't possibly have known there'd be an owl to sketch. That would be just too freaky.

Another shrug. "Tacey said you were working here this evening. When the café closed and you hadn't come back yet, I figured I'd come and see if you'd like some company for the walk home."

So thoughtful. Jakob would never have thought about doing something like that.

Rochelle tucked her arm through Ben's. "I'd love some company."

They weren't even halfway down Fairbairn Street before he asked, "What sort of work do you do inside the prison?"

Well, if there was one job to explain badly… "I pretend to be a convicted killer who was hanged over a hundred years ago."

Of course, Ben was shocked. He stared at her, and even in the ruddy glow of the streetlights, she could see the horror in his expression.

"For the tourists," she added, though this didn't seem to mollify him. Rochelle sighed. "The night time tours of the prison are done by torchlight, and they hire actors to jump out at the tour groups and tell them part of the prison's history. Most of them pop out of prison cells in the main cell block, or solitary, but they usually send me up to New Division, because there isn't much space in the Women's Division for a tour group, and I dress up as Martha Rendell, a woman convicted and hanged for the murder of her stepchildren. It didn't come out until much later that she was probably wrongfully convicted, treating the children under doctors' orders that the doctors denied, but by then, it was too late. She went to the gallows protesting her innocence – the only woman every hanged at Fremantle Prison. Makes you wonder how many of the other convicts came here convicted of crimes they didn't commit, because someone else with more power rigged the trial to blame an innocent for their actions."

Ben nodded gravely. "More than we will ever know, I suspect." He seemed to relax at this, content to keep walking.

"Have you ever been on one of the tours?" Rochelle asked.

"Played tourist inside a prison? No," Ben said.

From the way he said it, Rochelle suspected there was more he could have said, but he was deliberately holding his tongue. If she didn't know better, she'd think he'd been one of the prisoners here, but that wasn't possible. The prison had been closed for almost thirty years, since before she was born, and he didn't look any older than she did. Perhaps he'd been arrested for being drunk, or having a car accident. Or maybe he'd done something as a teenager and ended up in the juvenile justice system. Back in Scotland, maybe.

"I'll be working again Wednesday night. I could give you a tour, if you like – I'll leave a ticket for you at the gift shop." When Ben looked like refusing, she hastened to add, "We get all sorts on the tours. Sometimes even past prisoners and guards, who know all sorts of stories that even the tour guides haven't heard before. The stories this place could tell…" She shivered.

"I'm not sure whether to be amused or insulted that you think I could have been a prisoner here," Ben said. "Do I look like a criminal to you?"

And in that moment, she knew he'd done time, but if she said anything, he'd probably deny it.

"No, you don't," she said frankly. "But just because someone looks trustworthy or downright dodgy, doesn't mean they are. You tell me: am I making a mistake walking home with you?"

He grinned. "I swear on my life, that you are safe with me. Anyone who approaches us with the intention of making you feel unsafe…well, let's just say they might find themselves in danger, or at least discomfort."

She believed him. Which probably meant whatever crime he'd done as a teenager, it might have involved assault. But the sort where the victim might arguably have deserved it…

"Good," she found herself saying. "As long as you don't get arrested. Then who would walk me home?"

THIRTY-TWO

No matter how persuasive Rochelle tried to be, there was no way Ben intended to set foot inside that prison again. But as she grew increasingly suspicious at his refusals, rather than let her guess the truth, he was forced to say he would show up for a tour.

He could make his excuses when he arrived too late and missed the tour next week, but for now, she'd seemed satisfied.

He saw her safely home to the apartment

above the café, then headed to a nearby rooftop to make his way to the arts centre at the old asylum, as the life drawing class was being held there tomorrow. He might not be able to come out in sunlight, but he'd found a suitable spot in the ceiling above the room where the class was to be held, so that he could still join the class.

Ben took his time exploring the old building, losing track of time so that by the time he returned to the classroom, the class was already underway.

He didn't hesitate. He laid his sketchbook on one of the wide rafters, took a peek through the ceiling panel, and began to draw.

A figure took shape at the point of his pencil, a woman reclining on a dais, head pillowed on her arm as though she was sleeping. But the more he drew, the more familiar it looked. He'd seen this scene before. The way her arm stretched out, reaching for help she would never receive.

Oh God, it was Pamela.

The pencil shattered in his hand, now a million splinters that he deserved to feel stab into him, but they could not pierce his living stone skin.

Because the lady who reached across a hundred and seventy years for help, for justice, for vengeance…he had failed to give her any of them. Instead, he was drawing some other woman, drawn up in the same pose in which he'd carved Pamela, when he should be out there, hunting the man who'd killed his brothers, or the man who'd murdered her.

Not that he could leave the building yet – the sun still shone outside, though from the way it angled through the windows, in only a few hours he would be free.

He had time to waste on this picture, then, to pretend he was just another artist, instead of a vessel of vengeance.

His gaze swept the class. The stationery shop assistant had said there would be a variation of skill levels in this class, and she hadn't been wrong. One man could barely manage to keep his lines straight, for the box beneath the model. Others had drawn figures that looked vaguely human, and then there was one woman who'd drawn a man, not a woman, pointing at her with an accusing look on his face.

Ben blinked. There was another man on the page, and another. One had drawn a child, sex undetermined. There were women, too, but not one looked like Pamela. Yet when he looked at the model, it was her face he saw, a likeness so remarkable…

He turned to another page and began again. Then again.

Each time he began anew, the picture was the same. It was the statue of Pamela he'd carved into stone, then placed inside the folly he and Torstan had built for her father.

It couldn't be her. It couldn't be.

"We'd like to thank you for being our model for this class. Everyone, please show your thanks with a round of applause."

Ben glanced at the class. Everyone was putting their things away, as the model donned a sort of robe and headed toward a smaller room off the classroom.

Ben followed. He had to know. Perhaps she just looked like Pamela. A distant relative, a coincidence, there had to be some logical explanation that didn't involve Pamela coming back from the dead. He'd been convicted of her murder. Wished every day since that night that he'd been able to save her. If she was alive…

Ben stepped out of the wall, right into the room where the woman had now covered her nakedness with modern clothes. She turned around and…

…he smiled at Ben. "The hidden one emerges. Did you fancy your drawing so much you thought you would ask me on a date?"

A man. Ben was face to face with a man who looked nothing like Pamela, or any woman he'd ever known. This was…sorcery of some kind. Like the kind that had killed his brothers and allowed him to live far too long. This man could help him. Ben thrust the sketchbook in front of the man's face. "Explain this," he hissed.

The man took the sketchbook, leafing through the pages with his perfectly manicured hand. "Oh, this is truly lovely. You are quite talented."

Ben would not be diverted by flattery.

"Explain how I drew this, when I was looking at you."

The man let out a sigh. "People rarely go looking for the devil. Instead, they chase down their darkest desires and their deepest regrets, only to find they are unprepared when they come face to face with reality." He gestured down the length of his body.

Her body.

Ben found himself staring at a tall woman with Pamela's face, dressed in a modern black shirt and pants.

He blinked, and the man was back, his dark eyes smouldering.

This man thought Ben was a molly. That he wanted him. Or that he lusted after Pamela.

Ben shook his head. "I'm not chasing any of those things. I want to set things right. Things that might still be fixed." He could not bring Pamela back to life, but if he could at least avenge her…

The man let out a knowing laugh, as though he could read Ben's thoughts. If he was a sorcerer, perhaps he could. "If it's redemption you're after, that's very much a human thing.

You'll need to seek human help for that, as it's hardly the devil's speciality." He winked. "After all, not even the devil has managed to redeem himself yet, and not for lack of trying."

Wait…how had the talk turned to theology? Ben was no scholar, and certainly not one of the clergy.

The man reached into his pocket. "I'll tell you what. If you decide redemption isn't your thing, and you'd like something a little darker, with a side serving of vengeance, here's my card." He held out a shiny black rectangle between his finger and thumb. For a moment, his eyes seemed to be completely black, like he wasn't human, either. Then Ben blinked, and the man looked normal again.

Ben couldn't stop himself. He reached for the card.

The next thing he knew, the man was sauntering out of the room, into the now empty classroom.

Ben hurried to follow.

"May luck favour you and your new heiress, for young Pamela in your picture met her end long ago, and I'm sure has long forgotten about you and the life you know. If it truly is redemption you want, you must remember that redemption does not lie in the past, but only in the future." The man climbed into a black car as shiny as his calling card, and drove away.

Ben's breath caught in his throat. Not once had he told the strange man Pamela's name, nor what had happened to her.

He pulled out the man's card.

It read:

Luce Iblis

CEO

HELL Corporation

Beneath that was a long string of sixes. A phone number, presumably.

Of course, Ben would need to obtain a phone in order to call it, but he could do it.

Devils and darkness, vengeance and…

No. Ben tucked the card away. Maybe he'd look up this Luce Iblis, with his talk of devils, later, but he hadn't lied about wanting redemption. More than anything, he wished he could make things right. Justice more than vengeance.

But redemption was a human thing, Luce

had said. Almost as if he knew Ben wasn't human. Or that monsters were beyond redemption, much like devils.

Like called to like…though he was fairly sure Luce wasn't quite the same as Ben. The otherworldly aura of darkness that clung to him was something Ben definitely did not share.

But Rochelle was human, and he'd spent almost every night in this time trying to help her. Perhaps, if he were to ask for her help…she might…

She knew about history from a century ago. A woman wrongfully convicted of murder, a hundred years dead. If she could find one woman in the mists of the past, perhaps she could find three men. His brothers, and the man who'd killed them. If he found them, maybe redemption was possible, after all.

But if he wanted her help, he'd have to keep his promise, and turn up for that tour of the prison.

Fine. If that was what fate demanded, then he would do it. He would walk willingly into the prison he and his brothers had built and escaped from, and he would laugh and smile like any of the other tourists. It wasn't like any prison could hold him now. Especially not one made of stone.

And the devil, or whoever the mysterious Luce Iblis really was…he could wait. Because Ben had work to do.

THIRTY-THREE

Instead of going to the café when the sun set, Ben headed for the prison. The last daytime tour, one about the prison's convict past, was about to start, so he bought a ticket and joined it.

The tour guide, a silver-haired man whose name badge proclaimed he was called James, led the small group onto the parade ground, now covered in black bitumen, like the road outside.

"Imagine it's 1850. The colony is twenty

years old, with only a few thousand Europeans, all free settlers, and they wanted cheap labour. But no one wanted to come to Western Australia, and those who did couldn't afford it, so they wrote a letter to the British government, asking them to send convicts…"

A letter that resulted in them sending Dunstan's ship to Fremantle with a boatload of convicts. Ben, Tor and Dunstan would have been aboard as free settlers, and maybe Pamela, too, if she'd lived.

"They built this place using limestone quarried onsite, right here…"

Backbreaking work it had been, especially with the useless tools that had been sent over with them. Torstan had spent days in the blacksmith's shop, insisting the poor apprentice smith forge everything anew until he had what he needed. Or this prison might never have been built.

"They'd assemble out here, on the parade ground, every morning, to join a chain gang work crew…"

Ben shuddered. Chains had only been used for punishment detail when he'd been on those work crews. To have to wear chains every day…and he'd thought confinement to those tiny, lonely cells had been the worst they'd face.

Then the tour guide took them inside the main cell block…and pointed to the buckets. The toilet buckets.

What in heaven's name had happened to the plumbing? They'd put sinks in every cell, carving pipes out of wood when there wasn't enough metal. Ben hadn't gotten hands full of splinters, only for the prison administration to change their mind and start using buckets…no wonder there'd been riots like the ones the tour guide talked about. If Ben had been one of the inmates then, he might have led the riot himself.

Thank the Lord and fate and maybe even that bloody butcher for giving them the idea to escape.

As it was, he'd never been so happy to see that gatehouse in his life. He wanted to hurry out the gates and never look back.

Except… "Ben, you came!"

Rochelle stood in the courtyard, a beaming

smile on her face at the sight of him. A smile he wanted to return, even in this pit of despair.

"You didn't seem all that interested last week, so I haven't arranged for a ticket for you yet, but I'll do it now. I've got to go and get changed, but I'll see you inside, yeah?"

Ben found himself nodding.

Once more unto the breach…

Actually, the second tour was more bearable than the first. Perhaps it was because the tour guides talked about prisoners in later eras, during the time Ben had slept beneath the surface. Or perhaps it was the costumed actors, appearing most unexpectedly along the tour, to tell a dramatic tale of a moment in the prison's history, before disappearing once more.

He sensed Rochelle before he saw her, wandering the upper level before she surprised them on the stairs. She was dressed more like a woman of his time than the present day, and as she introduced herself as Martha Rendell, a mother with a most pitiful story, Ben began to understand why.

When Rochelle clasped her hands together

and cast her eyes heavenward, he almost believed she really could be Martha's ghost, and that every word she uttered was the truth as she said, "I am innocent before God and man of having done anything that injured the children."

Yet they'd convicted the poor woman, and hanged her for the murder of the children even as she proclaimed her innocence. Not the first innocent sent here to die, and not the last, either.

Applause from the other tourists jolted him out of his melancholy ruminations, but Rochelle had already made her exit, and he did not see her again.

The tour ended where it had begun, in the well-lit courtyard where he'd sat sketching the hunting owl last week. The owl was hunting elsewhere tonight, or perhaps the creature had not yet awoken and would not break its fast until later.

Ben settled down to wait.

He found himself watching the people instead, reliving their tours in animated tones with accompanying hand gestures as they strolled out the gates, not realising how lucky they were to be able to do so.

"Excuse me, sir, but we're closing. You'll have to leave."

Ben glanced up. One of the tour guides was definitely talking to him.

The woman locking up the gift shop flapped her hand at him. "No, it's fine. He's waiting for Rochelle. You can stay until she comes out. She won't be long."

Ben rose. "I don't mind. I can wait outside the gate just as easily as here, as long as you tell her where I am."

The tour guide and the shop woman fell into a vociferous whispered exchange over whether he should stay or go. Before they were anywhere near a decision, Rochelle made one for them.

"Hiya! What'd you think?"

"I almost believed you were her ghost," Ben admitted. "But I still can't believe how many tourists come to this place for entertainment."

Rochelle smacked his arm. "They come here to learn history in an entertaining way. It's not the same thing."

Ben bowed his head in acquiescence. "I'm sure you know far more about it than I do."

"Only about the women's prison, and the one archaeological field school I did back in first year, when I was trying for a double degree. Now, I'd just settle for one, if I can even manage that. I couldn't do the convict tour James said he took you on earlier. If anyone asks me questions about the prison's early history, I just point them at the convict database and wish them luck."

"A convict data base?" The words were familiar, but Ben had no idea what they meant all strung together like that.

"Sure. If it were still open, I'd take you into the Convict Depot, where they have displays of the original convict clothing and things, along with computers you can use to access the convict database. It's mostly used by people who think they might have convict ancestry."

He'd given her the perfect opening for a story that might actually sound plausible, without telling her the whole truth. "I had relatives who were convicts here, I think.

Dunstan and Torstan Stone. Can you find them in your data base?"

"Sure." Rochelle pulled out her phone, tapped at it for a moment, then frowned at the screen. "Okay, this might be better on my computer at home. When we get back to the café, you can come up and I'll search it for you, if you like."

How could he refuse?

THIRTY-FOUR

Rochelle was conscious of Ben's gaze on her as she waited for Octavia's computer to start up. She'd considered using her laptop, but Octavia had the most massive monitors hooked up to hers, so it would be easier to see.

The convict database chugged through its search, before finally the results flashed up.

"There were three Stones, not two," Rochelle said, scanning the screen. "They all arrived in Fremantle on the first of August, 1852, aboard the *William Jardine*. Torstan,

Dunstan and Ebenezer. Which ones did you say were your relatives?"

Ben looked thoughtful for a moment, then said slowly, "All of them. They were three brothers."

Rochelle shook her head. "Makes you wonder what their parents were thinking, giving them such names. I mean, there are whole pages of men called William and Arthur and Robert and John, and then there's these three…can you imagine being called Ebenezer? Everyone would call you Scrooge."

Ben coughed out a laugh. "Actually, I think you'll find Ebenezer Stone was born before Mr Dickens published his story, and in our family, it was usually shortened to Ben."

Rochelle sucked in a breath. She hadn't. Please, don't let her have… "Tell me I didn't just make fun of your name. I'm sorry, I shouldn't have said anything."

But Ben didn't look offended at all. He just stood there, grinning. "Ah, family traditions are hard to fathom, even when you're part of them. My mother was a great fan of Mr Dickens, and she read *A Christmas Carol* aloud every Christmas until she died, and then it fell to me. Even the greatest villain can be redeemed, she'd say, when my older brothers would joke about me seeing ghosts at Christmas."

"I'm sorry for your loss." The words came out automatically, but that didn't make them any less heartfelt.

Ben shrugged. "She was sick, and she was in pain. Death was a mercy to her, when it came."

"Yes." Rochelle closed her eyes, willing herself to see her mother before cancer had gotten to her, and reduced her to the living corpse she'd looked like in her final days. She swallowed. She was supposed to be researching Ben's ancestors, not mourning her mother. She aimed the cursor at the first record. "Let's check Ebenezer out first."

She stared at the record. Somehow, she'd thought this Ebenezer must have been Ben's ancestor. But he couldn't have been, and the screen before her knew why. "He died in June 1855. He was only twenty-one."

Ben nodded sagely, as if he already knew. "Yes, but what happened to the other brothers?"

Right. Those were the ones he'd asked about, not his namesake. "Ah. Right. Let's see. Dunstan's next on the list. An unmarried ship's carpenter, listed as literate, sentenced in Glasgow in 1850 for murder. Sentenced for life, and that's all."

Ben did not look happy. "Search for Torstan," he urged.

Rochelle clicked on the third brother. The only difference was his trade – Torstan had been a stonemason, not a carpenter. But still a murderer. Just like…yes, it said the same about Ebenezer. "There's nothing else here," she said. "I mean, for some of the others, you can see a death date, or a ticket of leave date, or the date they were pardoned. Ebenezer at least has a death date, but the others…there's nothing."

"Why not?"

Rochelle shrugged. "Well, maybe the records got damaged, or destroyed, or lost. And not everything got recorded, thought it should have been. Or maybe they just disappeared, and nobody knows what happened. In the first few years, when the prison was being constructed, the convicts slept in hammocks in a warehouse, where the Esplanade Hotel is now. There's a story that if they wanted to escape, all they had to do was sneak out the window and jump over the wall, and they could be free. Apparently the first place they went was to the pub, so all the guards had to do was wait until the pubs all closed, then go round them up again. Maybe these Stone brothers didn't go to the pub. Maybe they stowed away on a ship, or vanished into the bush, or…" She couldn't think of anything else.

Ben looked grim. "Or someone killed them and no one ever found the bodies."

She wanted to laugh, but he sounded too serious for it to be a joke. "Is that…the story you heard from your family?" Because colonial Fremantle had been a pretty backward place back then. Even Perth hadn't properly become a city until after the gold rushes started, and that was forty or fifty years later.

He gave a sharp nod. "I heard the man's name was William Pearse. He owned a butcher shop on High Street."

Rochelle shuddered. She had heard stories about murderers who sold bodies as meat to unsuspecting customers. What if this one had never been caught?

She asked Ben to spell the man's name, then entered it all in the search box and hit ENTER.

There were plenty of results, starting with some Fremantle history blogs and the state heritage register. She opened a few, then began to skim the articles.

"William Pearse arrived here in 1852 from Port Phillip Bay…that's Melbourne, and set up a butcher's shop on High Street. When his wife and children arrived to join him in 1855, he'd vanished." Just like the Stone brothers. "His wife and eldest son managed the business for some time, before they sold the property to a shipping business, which demolished the old building and built a new warehouse and offices in 1907. They called it Central Chambers." Rochelle's mouth had gone dry. She swallowed, but it didn't seem to help.

"Where is that?" Ben asked.

Rochelle didn't want to answer. If she did, it would make it true. That three men had been murdered metres away from where she slept at night.

But not saying anything wouldn't change the truth. She forced herself to walk to the window, and point at the building across the street. The one with the gargoyle on top of the large letters that proclaimed it as Central Chambers.

The building where the winged man had danced on the roof, not that many nights ago.

Ben stared in the direction of her pointing finger. "So close. All this time, I was so close," he breathed. Then he seemed to recollect himself, and bowed. "Thank you, Rochelle. You've been most helpful. I must go now, but I will see you tomorrow night in the café." He raced down the steps two at a time.

She trudged after him, knowing she'd have to lock the café doors behind him, but when she reached the doors, she saw they were already locked. And the back door was bolted shut.

Yet he'd definitely left.

Maybe he'd managed to deadlock the front door, and somehow pull it shut behind him. Yeah, that had to be it.

As long as it was locked. His relatives might have been murdered across the street by a serial killer over a century ago, but she still didn't feel safe unless all the doors and windows were locked.

If only the courts would hurry up and give her that restraining order so she could get Jakob out of her house, where she didn't have to worry about horrible historical happenings. Ugh, what if there were still angry ghosts hanging around?

THIRTY-FIVE

Standing on the street, outside the house that had replaced the butcher's shop, Ben forced himself to breathe. This is where it had happened. Where his brothers had died. Where he'd breathed his last. Where the guards had found him and carted what they thought was his corpse up to the Skinner Street cemetery, all those years ago.

The windows were all dark, but hadn't Rochelle said it was offices and warehouses now? The place would be deserted until daylight.

And Pearse's family had sold it to someone else, anyway. Wherever Pearse lived now, it wasn't here. He'd likely taken his ill gotten gold and found somewhere else to hide it.

What Ben needed was more information. Access to this line everyone's tablet and computer and phone seemed to be on, in whatever mystical way they managed it. For if Rochelle could find his brothers and Pearse on this line, then there surely were clues as to the butcher's current whereabouts, too.

He would start small, he decided, with a phone. Even school children possessed those, so surely the device would not confound him too much.

In the end, it wasn't the phone itself but the purchasing part that confounded him. The shop assistant required identification along with Ben's money, and whatever identity papers Ben might have had when he first arrived in the colony were surely long gone. Even if they weren't, he doubted the man behind the counter would accept papers that said he was over a hundred and eighty years old.

So he was forced to steal one. Well, sort of steal one. He'd found a shop that was closed for the night and taken a phone from the cabinet, then left enough money in their cash drawer to cover the cost.

Then he went up to an empty rooftop to open the box and do some research of his own. Only to discover that the phone screen was blank and would remain so until he had charged the battery, something which required electricity.

Ben sighed. Back to school he went.

THIRTY-SIX

"Is that your new boyfriend?"

Rochelle tugged the dress over her head so she could see who was speaking. Beth, one of the prison museum staff, and also possibly the most sunshiny person she'd ever met. "Who?"

"That young bloke who came in last week to do a tour with a ticket you'd arranged for him."

She wished she had a boyfriend as caring or as talented as Ben. "No, Ben's just a friend. He's the artist in residence at the café I work in, so he's kind of a colleague, if you could call Michelangelo's reincarnation a colleague when the only thing you have in common is that you sometimes work in the same place. He's the kind of guy who'd sketch or paint the most beautiful models and actors in the world, as they fall hopelessly in love with him, and he'd have his pick of them, if he only looked up from his work long enough to realise the look in their eyes is directed at him." Rochelle shook her head. "He's so down to earth…and at the same time, way out of my league."

"Don't sell yourself short," Beth chided. "You know, when I was with Brad, I thought like that, too, for a long time, especially after he cheated on me, but it was never about me at all. It was about him trying to get into the pants of as many women as possible. What you need to do is something wild and crazy to build up your confidence a bit. Like pole dancing. I know this great dance studio that runs classes…"

Rochelle burst out laughing. "I can't afford dance classes. I still haven't finished my degree, and I'm working this job and the one at the café just to pay the bills. Double the bills, seeing as I'm still paying all the bills for my house while my ex is still living there…"

"You should do something about that. He should be paying his own way, especially if he's your ex. You don't owe him anything," Beth said, echoing Rochelle's thoughts.

She'd get on that first thing tomorrow. Power and water weren't a huge issue, seeing as the solar panels kept the power bills down and they didn't use much water in winter because the garden pretty much watered itself in the winter rain, and they were a nightmare to reconnect, but she'd be damned if she kept paying for his superfast, unlimited capacity internet access when she wasn't using it. It wouldn't be enough to pay for dance classes, but maybe she could buy a new dress or something, come spring.

"Well, there is something wild and crazy that actually brings in money you might want to try…" Beth began, her eyes dancing.

"Don't even think about it. If I can't afford pole dancing classes, there's no way I could do it professionally. I'd only fall of my pole and everyone would laugh at me." She'd probably still do that in a class, come to think of it. Yet another reason why she shouldn't even attempt it.

"I meant life drawing classes. They run them up at the Fremantle Arts Centre, and they're always looking for new models. The only qualification you need is the ability to sit or lie still for extended periods, while people draw you."

Rochelle's mouth dropped open. "And by life drawing, you mean…?"

Beth nodded. "Naked, or mostly naked. In one of the classes, they were aiming for a sort of classical style, like something out of ancient Rome, so they had me draped in a length of filmy cloth. It was probably one of the most empowering things I ever did when Brad left me. All those people, devouring you with their eyes as they try to do justice to you with whatever medium they chose to work with. It's heady stuff. Makes you feel like an absolute goddess. In fact, I've heard some people find it addictive, wanting to model every week. They even offered me a mask to cover my face.

When I looked at some of the pictures afterwards, especially that ancient Roman one…wow, just wow. They made me look amazing."

Rochelle just shook her head. The thought of being naked in a room full of people and all of them staring at her…she couldn't imagine anything more embarrassing. "I couldn't."

Beth shooed away Rochelle's doubts with a wave of her hand. "I think you'd be surprised what you could do. Ask your friend. If the man draws like Michelangelo, he's had plenty of practice drawing nudes, and unless he's got a hundred eager apprentices willing to strip down like the Renaissance painters did, he'll have gotten it from life drawing classes. You might be nervous going in, but when you walk out of there, you'll feel like a goddess, I promise."

Rochelle forced herself to smile, when inside she was shuddering. "Thanks for the tip. I'll think about it. After I'm done with tonight's tours." She plucked at the black dress she wore when pretending to be Martha Rendell. "Because whether she was a murderer or not, I'm sure poor Martha was never a nude model for a bunch of artists."

Beth shrugged. "You never know. The newspapers at the time were full of reports about how immoral she was, for living with a man she wasn't married to, no matter how long he'd been separated from his wife. Maybe under those prim and proper clothes beat the heat of a woman who dared and bared all for those she loved."

"And they hanged her for it, protesting her innocence all the way to the gallows." Rochelle could only shake her head. Maybe Martha had wanted more out of life, but she'd never had the opportunity to reach for it, in between caring for her lover's kids and dying for them. "I'll think about it," she said again, as she hurried off to take her place along the tour route.

THIRTY-SEVEN

"Good evening. One cinnamon roll and a double shot espresso for my protector, as promised," Rochelle announced as she set her tray down on the table. He'd told her several times he didn't need anything to eat or drink while he was working, but he had admired the smell of the cinnamon rolls when she'd extracted them from the oven, and she'd gotten him to admit he liked his coffee black. "What are you working on?"

"Today's masterpiece," he said, holding up

the sketch.

"I do not stick my tongue out like that!" God, she looked ridiculous. And just a bit like a lizard.

"Sure you do. Whenever you're doing a design in the froth on top of a cappuccino, you stick the tip of your tongue out, just like that. I'm going to add it to the collection." He pinned it to the wall, next to all the other sketches he'd done of her.

Rochelle shook her head. "If you and Tacey hadn't sworn you were here to be my protector at night, I'd wonder if you're a stalker. I mean, that many pictures of me is a bit much." Kind of like that obsessive guy in *Amelie*. Only the way Ben did it, it wasn't so much annoying as endearing. And he even showed up to see her safely home on the nights she worked at the prison.

If she wasn't still sort of getting over Jakob, she might totally fall for the guy.

He shrugged. "When the café is quiet, and it's just you and me here, I take my inspiration from you. I believe I shall call today's piece BLEP." He scrawled the letters beneath the picture, and underlined them.

Until he went and did something like that.

Rochelle had to laugh. "You're a nutter, all right, but they do say great art requires at least a little bit of crazy. Ooh, look, we have a customer. For you or for me?"

He pulled out his portfolio. "For me, I think. I have a commission for him."

Rochelle returned to the counter, though her fingers itched to get her hands on that portfolio. He kept his best work in there, along with all the stuff he didn't display on the café wall. His little gallery had definitely grown in the time he'd been their artist in residence, but she hadn't seen much of his other work since that first night she'd met him, sketching the sunset.

She served a few customers, but her attention was on the exchange between Ben and the guy who was now gushing about how beautiful Ben's painting was. Then he turned it so Rochelle could see it and her breath caught in her throat.

In one hand, the guy held a photo of himself holding up a fish he'd evidently caught.

Ben's painting, while obviously the same subject matter, brought it to life like it was a film and not a photograph. You could almost see the fish moving, its scales sparkling in the sun, like it was the bloody Rainbow Fish itself, but determination steeled the fisherman's eyes, as he clutched his slippery prize, and you got the feeling if the fish made a desperate attempt to escape, the fisherman would probably dive right in after it. It was the final moment of a battle before victory was declared, but at this moment, it was still uncertain.

"Are you all right?"

She opened her eyes to find the customer had left, and she and Ben were alone in the shop again.

"I'm fine," she said. Just lost in a picture again. Why couldn't he draw her that beautifully? And calling it BLEP… "What did you call that one?"

"An Audience with the Spangled Emperor," Ben replied. "Because that's the sort of fish it was, and it managed to jump back in the water a moment after that was taken. The guy told me when he commissioned it, so that's what I painted."

Not just the photo, but the story behind it. Maybe that's why she could never capture emotion on film the way Ben layered it into his paintings. She could only take what was there. But Ben…he put part of himself into each painting, turning what you could see into something you could also feel.

If she had the money, she'd commission him to paint her. Not her sticking her tongue out and doing mundane things like making coffee but…something more. A picture of her not as she was, but what she wanted to aspire to.

"Can I see what else you've been working on?" she asked, her tone wistful. She didn't dare ask how much that portrait had cost.

"Of course." Ben set his portfolio on the table and opened it wide, beckoning her forward.

The sunsets she remembered, though he hadn't done any new ones. The owl he'd sketched over the gatehouse had been turned into a painting, with the feathers on its belly reminding her of some of the mosaics she'd seen in medieval churches in Europe. She hadn't seen that kind of detail when the owl flew over – just the shadow of its wings before it was gone. He'd done some night landscapes of the port, all lit up to load and unload the ships, lights reflecting off the water so clearly it was like the opposite of a Van Gogh painting.

And then there was…well, at first she'd thought it was another picture of the port, until she'd realised she was looking at trees and bushes, all decked out in fairy lights. A garden seen from high above, with tables and chairs dotted about the lawn, all empty and lit only by a thousand fairy lights…

"Where is this?" she asked. She wouldn't have been surprised if he'd said it was pure fantasy.

"It's the garden at the arts centre on the hill. The one that used to be an asylum."

Viewed from one of the upstairs windows, she guessed, unless he'd sent a drone up with a camera to get a bird's eye view. "It's beautiful."

He ducked his head. "You should see the real thing, though I don't think it's open to visitors at night, when they're closed."

"How did you manage to get in?"

"I have attended some drawing classes there that finished after dark."

And he'd gotten distracted by what he saw out the window and drawn that instead of whatever they'd been set. Still life, probably. A bowl of fruit or something. No wonder he'd drawn the garden instead.

"Have you ever done a life drawing class?"

God, where had that come from? She didn't even want to think about what Beth had said, yet here she was, blurting out rude questions.

"I have, most recently at the arts centre. They've brought in a few different models over the last few weeks, and it's refreshing to be able to draw the human form in its most natural state once again." As if in answer to the next question she didn't trust herself to ask without being even more rude, he pulled out several sketches of a woman's back and shoulders as she reclined on a couch, facing away from him, and laid them on the table. You could see every muscle in her arm, clearly outlined, as it rested along the back of the chair, and only when you got to her hand did you see why — she was nervous, her fingers tightly clenched around the decorative moulding.

Rochelle would be nervous, too, posing naked in front of all those people. She could barely believe Beth had been brave enough to do it.

"Have you ever had anyone offer to model for you?"

Oh God. She hadn't heard so many stupid things come out of her mouth since the last time she'd been drunk.

"Yes, back in Scotland. I lived in a small village, which didn't have life drawing classes the way Fremantle does now. So I was very lucky, otherwise all I'd have ever learned to draw was landscapes, and the occasional bird."

"Would you…would you paint me?"

THIRTY-EIGHT

"Would you paint me?"

YES, his heart and nether regions screamed, while his brain and his mouth were still floundering in shock that she'd asked him. He'd drawn her dozens of times, and she never seemed to like any of the pictures. He just wasn't good enough. After years of training, maybe, maybe he would be, but he still had a long way to go.

But if Rochelle was willing to take pity on

him, and let him practice…

He swallowed. "If you let me, I'd love to. I couldn't pay you as much as the art centre pays their models, so I understand if you'd rather…"

"Pay me? Don't your clients usually pay you?" She looked slightly panicky, as if she regretted the offer already. As well she might. If she hated his painting of her as much as she did the sketches, he was honour bound to pay her, even if only for seeing her own self represented so terribly.

"You've seen my work. It's never quite true to life, though I try hard to make it so. And some people I just can't get right at all. I mean, that guy today loved my sketch so much he insisted he wanted a painting of it, and I only charged him for materials. Materials enough for two or three paintings, mind you, in case he didn't like the first one and made me do it over again. I'm surprised he accepted the first one as it was. I mean, it was hardly true to life. His hands were not the same in the photo and no matter how much I tried, that fish just didn't come out the right colour…"

Her hand landed on his, silencing him. "That fish was beautiful. The whole painting was beautiful. If he hadn't liked it, you should have put it in a gallery for sale. I would have bought it, if I could afford it. As it is, with all the shifts I've been working here at the café and at the prison, what with not having to pay bills or much of my food, in another week or two, I might be able to scrape up enough to pay you what that guy did, so if you're willing to wait…"

Ben shook his head. "No, I'm the one who should pay you. I bought a phone last week, on top of everything I needed to paint the emperor, but if you're willing to wait until I've done another big commission or two…"

Rochelle laughed. "We're going to be here all night arguing, if we can't decide who's paying."

A customer came in then, interrupting the discussion, as Rochelle had to make several cups of coffee for the woman to take away, along with a box of cinnamon scrolls.

Ben wished he'd been able to eat the pastry she'd given him, instead of just enjoying the aroma, but he'd learned early on that his living stone body did not digest food, and the result of attempting to eat or drink anything was…messy, to say the least.

While she was distracted, he should probably toss his cold coffee into the pot plant, so she wouldn't notice he hadn't touched it.

Not a moment too soon – she was already farewelling the customer and on her way back.

"Okay, how's this for an idea. After the café closes on Monday, if you're free, you come up to my place to paint me. Octavia has a sort of chaise in her photo studio up there, with some really good lighting, so we can set up and go whenever you're ready. We go halves in the cost of the materials, so we're both paying, but if I really like the painting, and I want to keep it, I'll buy out your half so I can."

Ben considered her offer. It was better than he deserved. "All right, but if you like the painting, I'd happily give it to you. I'm getting a pretty good deal out of this anyway, seeing as I should be paying you and for all the materials, so it's only fair."

It was her turn to take her time, considering, but finally, she nodded. "All right. We have a deal. Monday night, then." She gave him a tremulous smile, and for a moment, she looked as nervous as he felt about the whole arrangement.

As though she had anything to be nervous about. All she had to do was sit on the couch and be her lovely self, something she did as easily as breathing, while he had to attempt to do her justice, first with a pencil, and then in paint.

He wasn't sure whether he wanted it to be Monday already…or if he'd prefer that Monday never came.

THIRTY-NINE

At least a dozen times a night, Rochelle decided she was going to cancel her Monday appointment with Ben. But every time she worked up the courage to cross the café to tell him, a customer would come in and distract her. So when Ben arrived on Monday, she knew she had to tell him.

But the moment he saw her, his face lit with a huge grin. "I've been counting down the hours until tonight. I have a new sketchbook and some new canvases, and I've bought enough paint so I don't run out. You won't regret this, I promise."

She managed to mumble something about how eager she was, too, before retreating behind the espresso machine.

But all too soon, Tacey's cuckoo clock chirped seven o'clock, and it was time to close the café. The quiet night meant she'd been able to do most of the cleaning before they closed, so all she had to do was lock the doors, turn the lights off, and take the remaining sandwiches to the fridge in the kitchen so she could have them for lunch tomorrow.

Then Ben followed her upstairs.

FORTY

Ben helped Rochelle lift the chaise into the middle of the makeshift studio, where the light was best, then chose a low plastic stool for himself.

"You should probably go change out of your work clothes. You won't want me to paint you in those," Ben said, though he knew full well it was not the clothes she wore that made her dislike the pictures he'd drawn of her downstairs. He was going to mess this up, he knew it, but some desperate hope kept him here, all the same. Because maybe, just maybe, he'd do a good job this time, and draw something that made her smile.

"All right." She vanished into the bathroom.

When she emerged, she wore nothing but a towel, and something underneath with cerise straps that circled her shoulders. Then the towel came off, and all he could see was her creamy skin, only slightly covered in cerise satin.

He'd never seen modern undergarments on a living, breathing woman before, and he had to admit, it was lovely. So little was covered, and yet it was more than enough to tantalise.

She bowed her head, following his gaze to her underwear. "It's the only matching set of underwear I have. They were on clearance because they're hot pink, but they looked okay when I tried them on, so I thought…"

"You look beautiful," Ben said, meaning every word. "So, you would like me to paint you in your underwear?"

Her cheeks turned as pink as her drawers. "Unless you want me to take them off." Still she wouldn't look at him.

He sighed. "Rochelle, I'm so grateful you would offer to model for me at all, I will paint you in anything you wish. Pink underwear. Martha Rendell's gown. Your work uniform. Or nothing at all. What I want most is to create a painting you like. So, what do you feel most comfortable wearing?"

She swallowed and raised her gaze to meet his eyes. "I want to take the bra off. The underwire is digging into my boobs something awful. No wonder they were on clearance. And if I'd realised the knickers were a g-string and not normal briefs, I never would have bought them. It feels like the string up the back is trying to saw me in half, bum first."

"Then take them off."

A pathetic pile of pink satin dropped to the floor, but she'd picked up the towel to cover herself again.

Ben winced. No way did he want to draw anything with that hideous frayed towel in it.

"How about you lie on the couch here, on your belly. Then bring your arms up, like this — one close and across your chest, and the other stretched out a little. Your legs…stretch them out behind you. Or maybe bend one knee, so your foot is up on the arm of the chair…" He demonstrated, then gestured for her to take her place on the couch.

The towel crumpled to the floor.

FORTY-ONE

Rochelle had never felt so exposed in her life, standing there in her underwear, and then only a towel, but Ben didn't stare like most men would. No, he just kept talking to her, like she was wearing her café blacks and not naked, as he explained how she should lie on the couch.

One arm here, the other arm there, and her legs…

She didn't think she had it right, but when she looked up at him, she found him nodding in approval.

"I like that. The way your legs are crossed at the ankle, raised up behind you. Now your hair. Would you let it loose, please?"

She ripped the elastic out of her ponytail and combed her fingers through her hair. She'd brushed and retied her hair before leaving the bathroom, but now she itched to have the brush in her hand again, if only to delay the inevitable.

"Shake your head, so your hair falls naturally over your shoulders and back."

Rochelle obeyed, and it felt…freeing, somehow. Which made absolutely no sense.

"Now look at me, like you want me to show you what I'm drawing."

She expected him to tell her to hold still, but the words never came. Instead, after several minutes, he would instruct her to change her pose a little. Shifting her hair to one side, over her shoulder, or down over her breasts as she sat up. Turning to face her body away from him, then glancing back over her shoulder.

Slowly, but surely, she began to relax. She forgot she was naked, doing what had to be the most outrageous thing she'd ever done, and more than once, she felt a smile on her lips, as Ben directed her to change her position again, before stopping her with:

"That's perfect!"

"Oh, lovely."

"Exactly like that."

After what felt like only a few minutes, but surely had been longer, Ben tossed his sketchbook and pencil onto the floor and rubbed his eyes. "I need a break. I imagine you do, too, after sitting still for so long."

Rochelle shook her head. "I could do this all night. It's fun!" But now she thought about it… "Maybe I could use a bathroom break," she admitted.

When she emerged from the bathroom, Ben didn't even notice – he was intent on his sketchbook, frowning as he added a few more lines to something.

"Can I see?" she asked, holding out her hand.

"Don't you want to put some clothes on first?" he said.

She should have, but now, after three hours…how could it have been three hours?

With the heating turned up, she wasn't even cold. Maybe she should walk around naked more often. Well, only when the café was closed, of course, and the blinds were down, and there was no one to see…

As if to remind her that there was still very much someone who could see her, Ben held out the sketchbook.

There were no tongues sticking out this time. He'd captured every pose he'd put her in, and made her look…like she was actually worth painting, instead of just a failed uni student turned barista who occasionally pretended to be a convicted killer to amuse tourists. Whose ex-boyfriend didn't even pay her enough attention to notice he'd been dumped. On these pages, she saw a woman with hope in her eyes, who might matter. Maybe not now, but one day, she'd be something to someone. Someone worth painting.

"Thank you!" She threw her arms around Ben's neck, and hugged him.

"Um…"

"Oh, right." She backed off and folded her

arms across her breasts. Maybe she should get dressed and make Ben a coffee or something. Share the last cinnamon scroll with him. "Can I get you something to eat or drink? What would you like?"

He closed his eyes. "With you standing there like that, the only thing I can think about is what you might taste like."

A sensible person would apologise, go put some clothes on, and let Ben leave before she embarrassed him any further.

But Rochelle didn't seem to be thinking straight tonight. There was something bold and daring about letting a man she barely knew sketch her naked, and she wasn't sure she was ready to go back to sensible just yet.

"Which part of me, exactly?"

His eyes darkened. "All of you."

FORTY-TWO

Rochelle's lips tasted sweet, but her tongue still held the bitter hint of coffee. Nor was she a novice at kissing, either – he could happily kiss her all night, breathing her in as he tasted and tasted and tasted.

But her breasts begged for his attention, so he kissed his way down her throat to the silken softness of her left breast, trembling slightly with each beat of her heart. He expected the pink pearl of her nipple to taste smooth and sweet, like her lips, but instead they were faintly salty…yes, both of them, for he was nothing if not thorough.

Rochelle moaned, throwing her head back, which pushed her breasts toward him like an offering, an invitation. One he could not refuse.

He carried her to the couch, and laid her on the red velvet, looking his fill as the light caressed her breasts, before he lowered his head for another taste.

Finally, he could stand it no more. He kissed his way down her belly, stroking her thighs until they parted for him. He breathed in her scent. Salt, yes, but something muskier, more earthy, too.

"Ben?" Worried eyes looked askance at him.

Had he gone too far?

"I want to taste all of you," he said.

"But I haven't…I've never…no one's ever…" Uncertainty crept into her tone.

"I've never done this before, either. Would you be willing to share your first time with me? I promise I will make it pleasurable for you." He knew how to give her pleasure, and he knew she would make it very clear if she did not enjoy his attentions. A gentleman would have taken her hesitation as his cue to withdraw, and maybe even leave. But Ben was no gentleman. He blew a warm breath between her legs, making her shiver, before he pressed his lips to hers again for a slow, languorous kiss.

She responded eagerly, her tongue ready to dance once more, but he still had one hand between her thighs, stroking lightly, ever upward, until he touched upon a spot that made her gasp. Then moan. Before she began to writhe beneath him, lifting her hips as if she wanted him to give her far more than just his calloused fingers.

"Let me taste you," he whispered in her ear, before swooping down and sucking hard on her nipple on his way lower still.

She was perilously close to release, so close he feared he would not be able to deny her that promised pleasure for a moment longer.

"Yes, oh yes!" she cried.

Not a moment too soon. Her orgasm burst like nectar on his tongue, for surely this was the wine of the ancient gods. Wine he must taste again and again, until he'd drunk his fill.

236

FORTY-THREE

Wait, was that his tongue? Or his fingers? Or both, twisting her insides until something inside her was about to…ohmygodohmygodohmyGOD…

When she could breathe again, no, when there was enough oxygen reaching her brain so she could think again, she knew for certain that had to be the finest orgasm she'd ever had. Actually, the first orgasm any man had ever given her, and Ben hadn't even taken his clothes off.

"I want more than your fingers and your mouth. Please, take me to bed, Ben."

His eyes regarded her wickedly from between her thighs. "But I'm not done tasting you yet."

Wait, he couldn't possibly give her another one? This soon after the first?

"Please, Ben," she begged as her breath grew short. Impossible as it was, he was about to….about to…"Ben, ohmygod, BEN, OHMYGOD!"

When she opened her eyes, the first thing she saw was him licking his fingers, that same wicked smile still on his face. "You have to be the most delicious thing I've ever tasted. I could do this all night."

She pushed herself up into a sitting position, and he backed up a little, though his hand didn't stop stroking her thigh.

So she reached down and did a little stroking of her own.

He was rock hard, and definitely ready for her. Bigger than she'd expected, too, though not uncomfortably so.

"I want to go to bed with you. I want this."

She gave him a squeeze, and his eyes widened.

Then they grew impossibly dark. "If you want me, then you shall have me."

He lifted her up, like she weighed nothing, and set her in the middle of the bed. He made short work of his clothes, so she scarcely had time to take him all in before he was climbing onto the bed, pushing her legs apart, until his hard length rested against her thigh, poised to grant all her wishes.

Condom. She didn't have any condoms.

But there was Octavia's condom collection. Surely she wouldn't miss one…

Rochelle opened the drawer of the bedside cabinet and fished about until her fingers closed on a foil packet. "Here." She tossed it to Ben.

He caught it, then stared at it. "What is this?"

Oh shit. It wasn't one of the really weird ones, was it?

Lime green, with hints of orange.

Not the alien one with the tentacles?

She breathed a sigh of relief as she realised it was just a ninja turtle one. The orange one, whatever his name was. "Here, I'll put it on for you," she said, ripping open the packet. So hot and hard in her hands…he'd feel even better inside her.

"There," she breathed. "Now, what ever happened to if you want me, you shall have me?"

FORTY-FOUR

The thin sheath was called a condom, he recalled faintly from something he'd seen in one of the health classes at the art college. An ingenious device that prevented disease and pregnancy, while not impeding sensation, as Rochelle had demonstrated as she'd rolled it up his length. Just the feel of her hands on him…it was almost enough to send him over the edge.

But she was wet and waiting for him. He didn't dare disappoint her.

She moaned as he entered her, her slick heat embracing him tightly, like nothing he'd ever felt before. Inch by glorious inch, he pushed his way deeper inside her, until he filled her to the hilt.

Maybe he had died, and this was heaven. It sure felt like it.

"Yes, oh, yes," she sighed.

He was supposed to move, wasn't he? He didn't want to. He wanted to stay here like this, buried deep inside her forever.

But then he did move, slowly out, before thrusting in again, her inner walls stroking his length far more thoroughly than her hand or his ever could. He wanted to savour every second of this, his first night with her. Finally, he understood why men were mad enough to marry, or take a mistress. To be able to enjoy the bliss of Rochelle's body, every night…heaven indeed.

"You can move a little faster, you know," Rochelle said. "You won't break me. And if you move faster, you'll come faster, too." A faint blush coloured her cheeks.

He waited until he was once again buried

balls deep inside her before he said, "And why would I want this to be over faster? Though you taste more salty than sweet, yours is the sweetest, most exquisite muff I have ever had the honour of entering. I mean to enjoy every moment." Realisation dawned, and he grinned. "Oh, but I will enjoy this even more if you were to come faster than me…"

He reached down and pressed his thumb against that little bundle of nerves that made her gasp, and began to grind against it, his gaze never leaving hers.

Her breathing grew shallow, her eyes glazing just a little as she let out a breathless whimper. It was all the warning he had before her inner walls began to convulse around him, squeezing him so tightly he feared she would trap him inside her forever, until she gave a little sob and a shudder and released him.

"Oh my God, Ben, that was…that was…" Her eyes shone with the words that she could not seem to say.

Or maybe it was because her breathing had grown shallow again, as he coaxed her firmly toward the next in many more orgasms.

"Come for me again," he commanded.

FORTY-FIVE

Rochelle lost count. Every time he purred, "Come for me," she could not help but obey, as if the combination of his fingers and his dick worked some sort of magic on her. Throughout it all, he did not let up his relentlessly steady pace, thrusting deep inside her just as slowly in and out as he'd begun. He might have given her more than a dozen orgasms, yet she hadn't given him a single one.

Maybe Jakob was right, and she was terrible in bed.

"Come with me, sweet lass," Ben said, his fingers slowing to match his thrusts now. "One more time."

She wasn't sure if her body could bear any more pleasure without exploding into a million pieces, but she could no more resist the pull of this next orgasm than she could resist gravity. For this one seemed to build deep inside her, overshadowing the pleasurable sparks where his fingers rubbed her clit. With every thrust, he was turning her core molten, into a volcano ready to explode.

She could not hold it much longer. Any moment, she was going to lose all control and…

"Come for me. Now."

She screamed his name as pleasure erupted all over her body, from head to fingers to curled toes.

This time, when she opened her eyes, she found him staring at her with the same sort of wonder in his expression that she felt.

"Did you…was it…?" *Did you finally come? Was it as good for you as it was for me?* She couldn't seem to get the words out. Maybe it was because he was still inside her, setting off aftershocks, though he wasn't moving any more.

Ben leaned down and kissed her. "That was the most spectacular sex I have ever known. I want to ask you to marry me right now, just so we can do that again."

Rochelle held her breath. If he asked, right now, she'd be mad enough to say yes.

He laughed, as if it was all a big joke.

Her heart plummeted. So this was only a one night stand, mindblowing though the sex had been, and they would likely never do it again.

She shifted, freeing her body from his so she could escape to the bathroom. "I'll just go clean myself up," she said with forced lightness, as the tears began to fall. Tears he could not see, for she was facing away from him.

FORTY-SIX

Ben instantly knew he'd said something wrong. In a moment, she'd gone from beaming, post-coital bliss to bursting into tears, though she'd tried to hide it well. Which meant he must have said something wrong. The question was…what? He'd complimented her on the excellent sex, then asked her to marry him. Neither were the sort of things that normally upset a woman, but women were mysterious creatures, after all.

He needed to make this right, but it was

hard to know how when he didn't know what he'd done wrong.

Unless it was because he should have proposed before indulging in such excellent sex…that might be it. He would just have to explain to her that a few hours hardly mattered in the overall scheme of things, or even a few days, for that matter, and he would happily become her husband if she would but name the date.

He folded his arms behind his head and stretched out on the bed, imagining bedding her again on their wedding night, and every night after.

She appeared in the bathroom doorway. Yearning burned in her eyes as she gazed at him, before their eyes met for only a moment, and she turned away.

But not before he saw her tears.

"Rochelle, wait." He followed her to the bathroom, where he found her standing before the mirror, splashing water on her face as though it might hide her tears. "I meant what I said. About wanting to do that again." Every night for the rest of their lives, he wanted to add, but caution told him to hold his tongue.

"That's the problem, isn't it? So do I. What girl wouldn't? When you look like…well, that." She waved her hand at his body.

He didn't need to glance down. He looked no different from any other man. Well, he was more wiry than Torstan, and a little shorter than Dunstan, but he was big enough to provide Rochelle with all the pleasure and protection she could ever need.

Unless the men of this time were more different than he realised…

"What do I look like to you?" he asked.

She let out a harsh little laugh. "You look like one of those statues in Rome. The ones of ancient heroes, naked in all their glory with cape and helmet and nothing else, standing proudly on their plinths for everyone to stare at in wonder. All muscles and mastery and mighty manhood. With your skills, you could make a fortune selling self portraits. Social media would go mad for you. I'm surprised you aren't already a social media sensation — you're a walking thirst trap. And then there's me. I don't know why you're so nice to me.

Why you persist in drawing me, when you know the pictures aren't going to turn out pretty. Why you'd bother to sleep with me when you could have anyone, anyone at all, instead of just me. And tonight was so incredible, no one else will ever be able to compare. So I'll spend the rest of my life, wishing for one more night with you."

No, Ben still didn't understand. "If you want me, you shall have me."

"But for how long?" She shook her head. "No, I've made a terrible mistake, and I don't know how to fix it."

He stepped forward, arms spread wide. "Then tell me what it is, so I can help you fix it."

She laughed. "I asked you to paint me, in the hope that you might see me as someone worth painting. That I might feel like that. And then I look at you, and realise I don't want a painting of me at all. I want a painting of you, just like you were on the bed a moment ago, so that I might remember this night, and the way you looked at me, and maybe one day I will see what you saw, that I will be someone worth painting."

"Then I will do dozens of sketches. Of our time together. And you shall choose the best of them, the one you like most, and I will paint it for you. Because you are someone worth painting, even if you cannot see it yourself. You're beautiful and kind and you see the world as a true artist, as anyone who has seen the effort you put into your coffee art will tell you. Tonight, you have allowed me to see your beauty in all its glory, to draw and maybe even paint you, before you became kindness itself and allowed me to share your bed, to touch and taste instead of just look. I cannot even begin to repay you for what you have given me tonight, which has been the best night of my life. I would happily spend the rest of my life, painting every moment of our night together, so I don't forget a single second."

She laughed through her tears. "God, that sounds awful. Spending the rest of your life painting me, when there are so many other things you could be doing."

"Then what would you have me do, to make you happy?" For he would do anything to chase her tears away. Rochelle should never cry for him.

"Well, in the absence of you spending the rest of your life painting me, or making love to me…I suppose I need to be realistic. I'd love a painting with you in it, and if we only have one night together…I'd like you to make love to me one more time, and then come to bed with me, so that I can fall asleep in your arms afterwards."

He would give her all those things and more, if she would only allow it, but he would start with the simplest thing first.

"Then lean forward and put your hands on the wall."

FORTY-SEVEN

"What did you say?" Rochelle turned around, so she was looking at his face and not his reflection. But he'd stepped forward so he stood right behind her, crowding her against the bathroom counter.

His eyes had gone dark again. "Lean forward and put your hands on the wall."

She did as he asked, which of course meant her backside pushed out behind her, where it met his once again hard cock.

He wrapped one arm around her breasts,

pulling her against him. "I said keep your hands on the wall."

She leaned forward again, planting her hands on either side of the mirror so she could at least fire a questioning glance at his reflection.

But he was looking down, not meeting her gaze at all. A moment later, she realised why, as the hard heat of him pushed between her thighs before thrusting deep inside her. Not slow like before at all.

Now his eyes were on her, capturing her gaze so she couldn't look away. "Before, you said you wanted me to take you hard and fast. A moment ago, you wanted me to take you back to bed, to make love to you. What do you want, Rochelle?"

He could see her soul, she was sure of it. She squirmed internally, which she should not have done, because with his dick so deep inside her, he surely felt it, too.

"I want you." The words burst out of her before she'd really thought them through, but they were true.

"And I want you, right here and now. Do

you believe me?"

His dick moved deep within her, rubbing against her most sensitive spots all at once, setting her insides on fire.

"Do you feel that?"

Mutely, she nodded.

"I'm hard for you, Rochelle, to pleasure you."

God, it felt like her insides were melting. How was he doing this?

"Do you know what I want?"

She wet her lips, though her mouth had become terribly dry. She hardly dared believe it, but she had to say it. In case it was true. "You want me." The words hung in the air, a whisper of power that could become a roar, if she only dared to believe him.

"I want you more than anything. Do you believe me?"

He didn't wait for an answer. Instead, he began to withdraw.

"No!" she cried, pushing back against him.

"You don't believe me?"

"I don't want you to stop. I want to believe you. I just..."

"Can you feel how hard I am for you? How much I want you?" He drove deep into her, not once, but over and over, fast and hard and oh it felt so good.

"Yes!" was all she could manage to say.

"Do you believe me now?"

"Yes!"

"Will you come for me?"

As many times as he wanted.

"Yes!"

"When you come for me, will you scream my name?"

"YES!"

He pounded into her, relentless as the waves against the sea wall in the harbour, and she surrendered herself to the sensation, body and soul, until the first orgasm ripped through her, and she did scream his name, not once, but over and over, until she was breathless. But Ben did not relent, and she had no wish for him to stop.

When he did eventually withdraw from her, heedless of her cries for him to continue, her knees buckled, for her legs were too weak to hold her up any more. Ben carried her to bed, laughingly pushing her hands away from his groin when she begged for more.

"You cannot fit a lifetime of sex into one night, lass, no matter how much you'd like to. We can do it again tomorrow, after you've slept. Now, rest."

With his strong arms around her, and her whole body thrumming from all the wondrous sex, Rochelle drifted off to sleep, her dreams filled with wondering how they might make love in the morning.

FORTY-EIGHT

The sun was well and truly up when Rochelle woke the next morning, and Ben was gone. On the pillow where his head had rested when she'd fallen asleep, he'd left his sketch book, with a sticky note on the front that only said:

See you tonight,

-B

He had the strangest handwriting – more like curly calligraphy than the sort of printing she'd use to scribble a note. Actually, the only time she'd seen writing like his outside of actual professional calligraphy was in the early prison records.

Ha. As an artist and a lover, he had superior skills that set him apart from everyone else. It shouldn't come as a surprise to her to discover he was an expert calligrapher, too.

Rochelle could hear Tacey clattering around in the kitchen downstairs, so the café must already be open. She should probably have a shower and open up the windows to get rid of the sex smell before she headed down to get breakfast.

Her nether regions were tender and aching, both inside and out, and she winced a little as she made herself wash thoroughly. Maybe she should do as Ben said, and not try to squeeze a year's worth of sex into one night.

But when the sex was so incredible, so irresistible, so damn addictive…how could she have stopped?

It wasn't just her private parts that had worked overtime last night, she discovered as her thighs burned all the way down the stairs.

Tacey was too busy to notice Rochelle's hobbling, as she flipped muffins out of their pans and stacked them all in the cabinet.

But a voice came from the other side of the counter, loud and clear: "Who have you been riding so hard he's made you bow-legged? I want his name and number."

Rochelle gave a little moan of relief as she hit flat ground. Her thighs didn't ache quite so much walking normally. Only then could she see who was teasing her.

Callie, Tacey's housemate and a lecturer at the university, grinned at her over a large cup of something. She had a pen and notepad and everything, which she pushed across the table toward Rochelle. "He's got to be good if you can barely walk after." Then she frowned. "Unless it was something not good and I need to cast a curse on someone. I know some good ones." She wiggled her fingers.

Rochelle was never sure if Callie was serious about witchcraft or not. Oh, she spoke Latin and was fluent in Viking runes, and she had an impressive collection of arcane books dating back centuries, but Tacey swore Callie wasn't actually a witch, because magic didn't exist, but she liked to pretend, especially when some of her particularly religious colleagues at the university made life difficult.

"No, I haven't heard from Jakob since I left him." Which was odd, come to think of it. Surely he'd have come to find her when dinner wasn't on the table. "Ben came to visit last night. He wanted to build his portfolio and I offered to model for him. So many poses…we were at it for hours."

"Oh, I don't doubt it." Callie winked. "So, did you go through much of Octavia's condom collection?"

Rochelle's cheeks heated. "I…"

Tacey smacked a muffin down in front of Callie. "Stop teasing her, or I'll tell her why you're here instead of at work. Ben's our artist in residence in the evenings at the café. If you want to meet him, come down any night. He takes commissions and he's evidently looking for more models to build his portfolio."

"And he's as virile as a bunny, evidently," Callie added, taking a huge bite of her muffin.

"Honestly. Right, you asked for it." Tacey turned to Rochelle. "Callie's here because her office is being exorcised for the second time this month because someone thinks she's been summoning mothman demons and releasing them in Fremantle."

Callie shrugged. "Can't summon what doesn't exist. I did find a good demon summoning spell, though. It'd be fun to try, just to see what happens. The ingredients looked like they'd be hard to find, though…"

"Well, as long as the spell doesn't involve toilet paper and hand sanitiser, maybe we should try it on our next girls' night," Tacey said. "Want to come?"

Rochelle shook her head. "I'll probably be working, anyway. You guys have fun. I'll…just grab a coffee and go back upstairs for a bit."

Ben's sketchbook was still on his pillow when Rochelle returned to her apartment. She might as well take another look at his work, seeing as he'd probably ask her tonight which one was her favourite.

She leafed through the pages, admiring his work but wishing it didn't all look like…well, her. Ordinary and awkward and not the slightest bit sexy. When she reached the last one, she sighed. If only Ben had drawn a self-portrait like she'd asked…

She took a big gulp of coffee as she flipped through the remaining pages, not quite daring to hope as she looked anyway.

The first sketch she saw made her spit her coffee out, spraying all the way across the table. Rochelle rushed to clean up the mess before it could drip onto the floor.

Thankfully, she'd missed the sketchbook, which she didn't pick up again until she was certain the table was clean and dry.

What she saw this time made her mouth drop open, but as it was empty this time, she forced herself to keep turning the pages.

She'd never seen anything so erotic in her life. Nope, not even in one of Jakob's pirated porn films. This was…well, it had to be her, but…

A pair of breasts, cupped in a man's hands. Two legs spread wide, showing…that couldn't possibly be her private parts, could it? Then several more of the same pussy, with a man's hands glistening with moisture as he fingered, stroked and teased the lucky woman.

Rochelle turned the page. Two more

sketches from the same angle, only this time you could see more of the woman, arching her back and crying out as the man's fingers plunged deep inside her, and her hand clutching the sheet in either desperation or ecstasy.

His penis, resting against her leg, readying to enter her glistening depths. Rochelle wasn't sure how Ben could make a simple pencil sketch glisten like that, but somehow, he'd managed it.

Below it, his penis again, dripping wet as he withdrew from her, and on the next page…yes, that was her all right, hands fisting the sheets as she stared rapturously at Ben, who was buried so deep inside her you could only see a hint of his shaft through his hair.

Then two whole pages on just her face – the expressions she'd evidently worn while he was…while they were…while they'd bonked like bunnies, to use Callie's animal imagery.

She didn't look too bad in these ones, she had to admit. Wide, dreamy eyes and a blissful smile suited her, or maybe Ben had just made her look prettier than she was for these.

Because these were surely the results of all the orgasms he'd given her last night.

After the gallery of her pulling faces, he'd decided to draw them having sex in the bathroom. The first few pages were vignettes, closeups of…well, his penis and her bottom, mostly, as even with her leaning over, her private parts hadn't exactly been in full view. But then there were the pictures in the mirror, which she'd been too busy paying attention to last night.

Her hands, clenched around the mirror frame.

His hands, clutching her breasts as he'd pounded into her.

Her blissful expression, mouth opening as though she was singing some variation on hallelujah, when she knew she'd been screaming his name.

His reflection in the mirror, from about the waist up, all chiselled muscle in deep shadow, and his face even more shadowed still as he stared directly at her. The desire in his eyes…

Rochelle gulped. She was pretty sure her underwear was soaked through, if they hadn't melted entirely, and all she was doing was looking at a pencil sketch of his reflection.

How would she manage to work in the same café with him without throwing herself at him? Work tonight was going to be torture.

She turned the page.

Oh. My. God.

"Hey, Rochelle? Are you coming down to mind the café while I take Rory to school? Just that you said you'd be down an hour ago, and if we don't leave now, she'll be late."

Rochelle blinked. It took her a long moment to tear her eyes away from the image, but she managed it…barely. Even as she made her way down the steps, the image remained branded to the back of her retina, like she'd stared at the sun too long.

"Two cappuccinos and two macadamia muffins, coming right up."

No wonder he'd drawn so many of those vignettes. He'd wanted to get all the details right.

"Here's your espresso, sir. Oh, don't forget your afghan cookie."

Then he'd painstakingly assembled them

into one amazingly detailed picture that…

"Let me just check I have this right. One caramel macchiato with soy milk, one oat milk mochaccino, a Vienna chocolate with coconut milk and coconut cream, one dirty chai and two flat whites with skim milk. And for the food…six bacon and egg cups, three gluten free, three wholemeal, plus three chocolate muffins, one blueberry and two of the raspberry friands. Did I miss anything?"

Ben hadn't. She could have stared at the sketch for hours, drinking it all in. She had stared at it for at least an hour, according to Tacey. Good thing Tacey hadn't come upstairs and actually looked at it…

"I'm sorry, ma'am, you said you want five babycinos without the froth? You know that's just milk, right?"

It was just a picture, for fuck's sake. A pencil sketch that captured the vaguest representation of a moment in time that even she couldn't remember that clearly.

"Right, so that's five babycinos with no froth, and two Vienna chocolates with skim milk. And two slices of the devil's own cheesecake. Did you want these to dine in or take away?"

It made her want to go buy a vibrator. Because just thinking about that picture, let alone looking at it, made her ache with longing to feel him inside her again. Except how could a machine feel anything like a living, breathing, thrusting human?

What she really wanted was a big box of condoms, and Ben in her bed forever. Was that so wrong?

"Sorry I'm late. There was an accident out the front of Rory's school, and two mothers screaming in the middle of the street, blocking off all traffic, as they both blamed each other for the accident. They were both driving down the middle of the street, though, so it's anyone's guess. The police had just arrived when I finally managed to get out of there." Tacey tied on her apron. "Now shoo. Go do an assignment or catch up on sleep or wash your sheets or whatever you do until you start your shift at five o'clock."

Well, she could go buy some condoms. Ben would be back tonight, he'd said, and if there was one person she could rely on, it was him. He'd been nothing but honest with her since the day they met.

Hadn't he?

FORTY-NINE

For a Tuesday night, the café was unusually busy. Rochelle hadn't had a chance to give him more than a nod of greeting from across the room as she served customer after customer and brewed an ocean of coffee. Even when the clock chimed seven, there were still customers sitting at the tables, so Rochelle had to clean up around them, and it was another hour before she could close the café completely and turn the lights out.

She was dead on her feet, using the broom

for support, when she finally came to his table.

"Did you see my sketches? Do you have a favourite?" Ben asked eagerly.

A rosy blush coloured her cheeks. "Yes, but…I want to discuss it with you before you turn it into a painting. Upstairs."

"Lead the way," he responded, only too happy to follow her.

The book lay closed on the table, and she clutched it to her chest for a long moment before she began. "Look, your drawings are…lovely. Very detailed."

Ben nodded. He prided himself on the accuracy of every anatomical detail, especially for sketches of this nature. The better they were, the better he'd been paid for them – at least in the past.

"The more I looked at them, the more I got to thinking. You've evidently drawn a lot of people in a state of undress. Yet you told me once there weren't any life drawing classes where you used to live in Scotland. So if you weren't drawing models…am I just the last in a long line of conquests, women that you sleep with and then sketch, and that's why you only give them one night, because once you've taken their likeness, you're not interested any more, and you move on to someone else with different shaped boobs or a more interesting face or…" She swallowed. "Am I just a body to you? Somebody you can order about and pose like a doll, so that you might draw an interesting picture, and that's all? How many women like me are there?"

He wanted to laugh, but that would not be fair. It wasn't Rochelle's fault he hadn't told her.

So he said, "I swear to you, there are no women like you, anywhere. At least not that I've met. You are the only woman I have ever entrusted with my sketchbook. But I will not deny I have had a great deal of practice drawing naked people." He sighed. "If you wish to know the truth, which I believe you deserve after last night, then I will tell you two secrets that I have never told anyone. But only if you trust me, for we are alone here tonight."

She began to laugh. "Why wouldn't I trust you? We were up here alone last night, and I never felt unsafe for a moment."

Either times had changed, or Rochelle truly was unique in her view of the world. "Last night, I persuaded you to strip naked, permit me to draw your bare body, before I stole your virtue, then took my pleasure of you not once but twice, before spending the night in your bed. Back home, that would have your father threatening to come after me with a horsewhip."

She frowned. "I think my father has a bullwhip on the station, and probably a collection of riding crops, but I can't recall the last time anyone actually used one of them on any of the stock, let alone a person. That's barbaric. As for virtue…by which I think you mean virginity, that boat sailed a long time ago, when Jakob and I were still at high school. I'm not sure I have any virtue left to steal. As for the pleasure you took, I'm pretty sure you gave way more than you received, so if we're keeping score…I probably owe you. But the drawings and the secrets…yes, I would like to know the truth, please. Because half of me wants to drag you to my bed and have my wicked way with you all night, while the other half is screaming about how little I know you."

Ben ducked his head. "Very well. Then my first secret is that I had never lain with a woman until last night. The most I had ever done was kiss a girl, and that was a very long time ago, back in Scotland."

Her mouth dropped open. "I don't believe it. You were…you knew my body better than I did. You made me come so many times I lost count, and that was before you even got naked. You can't possibly have been a virgin yesterday."

"Yet I was. You might say my knowledge was all theory and observation, with no application, until last night. I drew a great number of pictures afterward, because I could not sleep. Could not stop thinking about the delightful feel of your body twined about mine, and I did not want to forget a single moment of our night together. But I realised after I drew them that those pictures might be compromising to you and to myself, which is why I left it with you, for I know you will keep it safe." A pity he had not thought to keep his other sketchbooks hidden back in Scotland, but he had been young and naïve then, and he would not make the same mistake again.

"That's why…you wanted to taste everything, and take the first time so slowly. Because it was your first time. But the second time…" Her cheeks turned pink again.

"The second time I did not hold back." Ben grinned at the memory. Rochelle had not held back, either, and if she was willing to let him share her bed again, he hoped their third time would be even more pleasurable for both of them.

"So you believe my first secret, now?" he pressed.

Rochelle nodded. "I think so, yes. I'm ready for the second one."

No, she probably wasn't. He wasn't sure he was ready to tell it. But before there could be a third time, she needed to know. For he had no right to keep such a secret from her.

FIFTY

Ben took a deep breath. "Back home, there weren't many art classes, at least not ones my family could afford, so I drew whatever I could. Borrowed books on drawing. Until I was late coming home from school one day and I went past the pub. We had two pubs in the village. One in the middle of town, and one on the edge, along the road to Glasgow. Anyway, it was getting dark, and there was a bit of a party going on at the edge tavern. A man and a woman were half hanging out the window, naked as the day they were born, just like some of the pictures in the Italian art book I'd borrowed.

"Now, I didn't know they were having sex at the time, but I was so eager to draw them that I took out my sketchbook and pencils and…well, one of the pub staff saw me and tried to shoo me away, but I explained why I wanted to draw them, how the couple looked like a religious painting I'd seen in a book. At this point, he was laughing so hard he could scarcely speak, as he dragged me inside to see the manager. Not the manager, but actually the brothel madam, I later found out.

"She found my story funny, too, but she also knew my mother, and she felt that if my mother were not about to educate me about such matters, then she would take it upon herself."

Rochelle let out a horrified cry. "That's horrible! How old were you?"

Ben shrugged. "I was about ten or twelve. Old enough to know where baby sheep and cows come from, and, she said, old enough to know what husbands do to their wives, as well as their whores. So she took me through the secret passageways of the place, right up to the attic, and showed me all the peepholes, so that I might see what really went on. How it was nothing like religious art, and in some cases, was about as wicked as could be.

"But I was just a boy, and I found it fascinating. I later discovered the painting I'd seen was actually a depiction of hell or judgement or some such, which explained why it had so many writhing bodies, but that didn't change my mind. If I could learn to draw these people, then maybe I could become good enough to paint on the walls of churches, or at least that's what I thought. So I asked the madam if she might let me draw what I saw. I suspect she thought I would tire of it soon enough, so she agreed.

"I saw all manner of things. Bodies of all shapes and sizes, in countless different positions. I learned to draw fast, to capture a person in as few lines as possible, as I could flesh the picture out later, as it were. I learned to draw faces in every expression imaginable. To the madam's regret, I did not tire of her establishment at all.

"One night, a man beat a girl so badly he broke her arm, before he ran out of the place without paying. Two of the inn's men went after him, armed with my sketch so that they could identify him. While the madam never told me the details, she did say that they'd never have caught him if not for my picture, and I was permitted to spend as much time in the brothel's secret passages as I wanted.

"My brothers were off working at their apprenticeships by then, and with my mother gone, Father spent all his time managing the small farm where we lived, so no one cared if I spent every afternoon in the brothel, as long as I came home for dinner, which of course I did.

One day, I saw a man sitting in the parlour, leafing through some picture books I'd never noticed before. When the room was empty, I sneaked in and took a look for myself. The pictures were the erotic kind, with a great deal of attention paid to the bodies of the people in them, and very little to their faces. I asked the madam about them, and she said they were printed in London. She even showed me the address. So when I had a few coins to spare, I wrote a letter to the printer, enclosing some examples of my work.

"'The reply came quick – there was money in the envelope, and a promise of more if I could send them other sketches just like them.

"'From that moment, I began to see a future I had not dared to dream of before. One where I might have the money to attend art school in Italy, if I could only sell enough pictures.

"'Some nights, they hosted an illegal boxing ring, where the fighters were as dirty as their tactics. The reigning champion, an Irishman who went by the name of Russian Vlad, taught me to fight over the years. I even ventured into the ring once or twice. The prize money was not much, but the trick was to bet on myself and make sure the odds made the other man look far more likely to win, because when I won, the wagers were where the money was.

"'I'd almost made enough money to pay for my passage to Italy when my father died. My brother had finished his apprenticeship then, so he took me on as his apprentice. We moved around a lot, wherever the work was, but it was steady work, and I still found time to draw.

"I was friends with a girl, an artist like me, only she'd had lessons and everything. She painted the loveliest landscapes. Watercolours, mostly. Anyway, she got hurt, and the police arrested me as a suspect. When they searched my house, they found my sketchbooks, and took them as evidence. They said the pictures were of her, or what I imagined she looked like, though they looked nothing like her, and they were proof that I had planned the terrible things she suffered. They sent me to prison."

He half expected Rochelle to recoil in horror, but the only movement she made was to wipe her tears away with her hands. "Oh, Ben, I'm so sorry. Your friend…was she…all right afterward?"

Almost as if she knew.

"She died."

Rochelle nodded, as if she'd expected that.

"I never touched her. Not that night, or any other. I'd never even kissed her, though I would have, if she'd asked me to. And they never did catch the man who did it."

The man was likely dead now, out of reach. Rotting in hell, hopefully.

"I behaved myself. Did my time, so as soon as I could, I managed to come to Australia, where I've been trying to build a new life. But even though I'm half a world away, it's like she still haunts me. Because even if I wasn't the one who killed her, I wasn't there when she needed me. I said she could come to me for help with anything, and the one time she did…I wasn't there."

FIFTY-ONE

Rochelle bowed her head. She hadn't wanted to be right, about him spending time in a juvenile prison, but she couldn't have guessed that he'd be sent there for a crime he hadn't committed. That was just…horrible. How anyone could have… Surely there would have been DNA evidence of the real culprit. Forensics could have found something. She opened her mouth to ask why…

But one look at his bowed head, his slumped shoulders…she closed her mouth again. She couldn't say any of it. Somehow along the way, this amazing man had made peace with the horrible injustice that'd been done to him and here he was, trying to make a new life. The sort of life he deserved.

Realisation dawned at how a man like Ben could still be a virgin.

"You haven't drawn or gotten close to anyone since she died, have you?" Rochelle asked, almost afraid of the answer.

"Not until last night with you."

She wasn't sure whether to be horrified at how much he'd suffered, or honoured that he'd trusted her enough to share his story with her. To share everything with her.

Rochelle threw her arms around Ben's neck and hugged him. His arms closed around her, returning the embrace. They might have stood there for an eternity or only a moment, she did not know, but when they parted, it was only so that she could see his face as she said, "I know which picture I want you to paint." She flipped to the final sketch and stroked her hand across it. "This one. I only have to glance at it, and I can feel it, feel you, as though I was there. I would give anything to feel that again, even if it's just a memory."

Ben snorted. "Even now you know you had sex with an ex-convict, who by his sixteenth birthday knew more about sex than any whore alive, though I'd never done more than kiss a girl?"

"You could have fooled me. Last night was incredible." Rochelle untied her apron, then let her pants and underwear slide to the floor. "Your past doesn't change anything. It's not who you are." She pushed him down into a chair, then straddled him. She could feel him, hot and hard between her thighs. She pulled her shirt over her head, then reached back to unhook her bra.

"You're mad. I just told you I'm a convicted killer, and you still want me?" His hands flew up, hovering over her skin, but not quite close enough to touch. Like he didn't trust himself.

"But you didn't kill her. You might not have saved her from the man who did, but you didn't kill her." No wonder he was always so gallant, wanting to walk her home. Rochelle closed her eyes and began to grind against him, wishing he was naked, too.

"No, but…how can you stand making love to a monster?" He stabbed a finger at the picture of them together last night. He did look dark there, almost like he wanted to devour her. If only he'd look at her like that now…she'd come on the spot.

"Um…in just one night, you gave me more orgasms than I've had in years, sleeping with Jakob. And every single one of them was better than anything I've ever felt before. If that's what making love to a monster is like, then you've ruined me for normal men for life. I only want monster cock from here on in." She reached into his pants for the member in question, and together they shuffled his pants off so he was naked from the waist down. His shirt sailed across the room, where it would no longer get in the way, as she raised herself up just enough so that in one thrust, he'd be inside her.

Oh, wait, they still needed…

"I bought condoms," they both said as the same time, then laughed.

Rochelle dug out the biggest box she'd been

able to find and held it out.

Ben's box was smaller, but the pictures were a lot more…holy hell, they hadn't sold those in Coles.

"The lady in the shop said these would give you the most pleasure. I promised I would return for more if they meet with your approval," Ben said, but she wasn't listening. She was too busy reading the description on the back of the box.

"Ribbed…with a little extra…" Her mouth was so dry, the words just wouldn't come out. So she ripped open a packet, and rolled it down his length. She had to stop to admire the result. "Wow. I've always dreamed of doing a guy with a ribbed cock, but I never thought it would actually happen." She might have been imagining it, but the ridges seemed to bulge out even more as she stared at him, licking her lips. "Ben, I want…no, I need…"

He grabbed her hips and pulled her into his lap. He filled her with one perfectly aimed thrust, and she was soon far too busy focussing on the sensations rippling through her body to say another word.

FIFTY-TWO

He made love to her until she was thoroughly sated. Perhaps a little too thoroughly, for her even breathing as her head rested on his chest seemed to say she'd fallen asleep. Reluctantly, he pulled the covers up over them both, for he had no intention of letting go of this amazing woman, at least until dawn forced him to.

Such fragile strength demanded his protection, despite the demands from his brothers' shades for vengeance. His brothers had waited for more than a century – another day, another week, even another decade would make no difference.

If he'd known how addictive he would find the soft yielding of her body as she embraced him, all of him, both the monstrous and the good, and the sweet sound of her cries of pleasure that only he could elicit from her, roaring to a crescendo as she screamed his name when she reached her peak.

Even now, as she drifted into sleep that her fragile human body surely needed, he wanted to kiss her awake, slip his fingers between her thighs, and caress her into a state of shuddering bliss.

But he resisted. The sooner she surrendered to her dreams, the sooner he could start work on her painting, perhaps the most erotic work he had ever created, for unlike the hundreds of sketches he'd done of other people coupling, this was him and the woman he loved, with so much feeling infused in every stroke of his pencil as he'd stroked into her, over and over and over as she begged for more. Because, against all odds, Rochelle wanted him, and only him.

Perhaps he should find that man's calling card, that Luce Iblis, and set him on the search for the butcher instead. Let the creature of darkness seek vengeance for his brothers, leaving Ben free to love Rochelle, and live.

Where was the card? He'd tucked it into his sketchbook, surely.

Carefully, Ben slipped out of Rochelle's embrace, and padded to the table, where he'd left his satchel. He'd gone from one sketchbook to a dozen, straining the bag's seams. Soon, he'd have to leave some of them behind when he came to the café, for the bag would not hold them all. Perhaps Rochelle would agree to keep them safe for him. As long as nothing untoward happened to her…

As if he'd summoned her with a thought, her warm body slid into his lap, rubbing against him in the most tantalising way, as though she was not as satisfied as he'd believed.

"What are these? Oh, are these the sketches from your life drawing class?" She leaned forward for a better look, heedless of the way that pressed her bottom harder against his groin. "Wow, you really are a talented artist, you know that? All your practice paid off. I bet this girl actually isn't half as beautiful in real life as you make her out to be in your drawings. I mean, look at how good you made me appear. And this one…" She flipped the pages back until the first sketch came into view, the one of Luce Iblis looking like Pamela. It had been an illusion the other man had created, not a figment of Ben's own imagination, he knew now.

What would Rochelle see when she looked at it?

She was frowning, like she did when she looked at some of the pictures he'd drawn of her in the café. That wasn't good. "I've seen this before. Were you drawing a person posing to look like the statue, or the statue itself? The statue was amazing work, I've never seen anything quite like it. I'm not surprised you sketched it." She reached for her phone, then swiped across the screen several times before she held it out to him. "I did a whole series of posts about it when I was travelling. I had high hopes of becoming a travel blogger of sorts, until Jakob and Mum's illness summoned me home. Ah, here it is. A lonely line of cliffs, with nothing but ruins along them now, but in the middle of the fallen stones is this statue, guarded by three fierce looking monsters. There are all sorts of stories – that it's a grave, and the white lady's ghost walks the ruins, looking for her lost love. That it's a gift from the fae, for some favour no one seems to be able to say. Here, look."

Ben didn't want to, but he could not refuse, either. The white limestone he remembered had weathered to grey, giving the block of stone more shadows than it had cast on the day he carved it. Yet there she was, veiled and reaching for him, the same as the day he'd met her. A face he would never see again.

"Did you see the ghost with your own eyes?" Ben asked. Perhaps, if Pamela still haunted those ruins, he might be able to see her again.

Rochelle gave a most unladylike snort. "No, though I camped out in those ruins for a whole week, hoping I might. I heard plenty of howling, which the locals swore was a different ghost, the restless spirit of the last lord of the castle, but I'm sure it was just the wind. It's weird, though. The statues – the girl, and her gargoyle protectors – were in such good condition, while the castle crumbled around them. Yet the stones looked identical. I looked, but I couldn't find any photos of what the castle looked like intact."

"That's because it never was. The castle those statues stood in was a folly, a fake ruin created for the knight who ruled those lands, a man with more money than sense. Until he gambled that away, or so I heard." From Pamela's own lips, as she wept at the betrayal of her own father, who meant to sell her to settle his debts. He should have persuaded her to run away with him that very night. Then she might not have died…

"No, that's not true. There was a castle. The men in the tavern were very insistent about it, for the last lord burned it when he took his own life." Rochelle took the phone from him, swiped at it, then handed it back. "There. They say he burned himself alive in that tower."

Even burned and half collapsed, Ben would

recognise Burke Castle anywhere. "It wasn't really a castle. Just a tower, which is why he wanted the ruin built that looked like a much larger castle had once stood there. The tower was Burke Castle, but the ruined stone walls where the statues are? That's Burke's folly."

"Well, that's not the story they tell in the village pub. There, they say the lord went mad when his daughter died. That they caught the murderers, but the lord kept insisting they'd got the wrong man, and the real murderer was in London, free as a bird, and he meant to catch him himself. Then he disappeared for a while – likely headed down to London, they said – and when he returned, he'd changed his tune. Now, he kept saying the bird had been killed, butchered like he deserved, but justice still needed to be served. The innkeeper and his men tried to stop him, but the lord was having none of it. He took two bottles of their best brandy and rode home. When the sun rose, the lord's castle was a burning inferno, and they later found his body among the ashes. Only thing was, there were two heads. They ended up burying both in the same coffin, because they didn't know which one was his. I'm sure I wrote his name down somewhere…"

"Sir William Burke. Not a lord at all, only a foolish knight who gambled too much." Ben wondered whose head the other one had been. "I hope the other head belonged to Brandon, and that he did get what he deserved."

"Brandon? No, the lord's name was Burke, I'm sure of it, because it was so close to my own last name. Well, different spelling, but still. I was curious. There might have been a family connection."

Ben shook his head. "Trust me, you did not want to claim any kind of relationship with Sir William Burke. He sold his daughter to a London moneylender, a man named Brandon, and he's the one who killed her, or that's what I heard."

Rochelle stared at him for a long moment. "You're from Scotland. You actually know this story. Not just the dramatic version they sell to tourists, but what really happened. Did you live near there?"

"For a time. But it was a family tale. We

were not family to the Burkes, of course, for my family were mostly farmers and tradesmen. No, it was the men convicted of the murder they did not commit – the Stone brothers, transported here. A good place to make a new life, or so they say."

"The convicts you wanted me to look up. That was…that was them? And that's why you came here after you were released. Because if your ancestors could make a new life here, then maybe you could, too…my God, Ben, that's horrible. History repeating itself when it should never have happened the first time. I can't believe…"

"Can you find out what happened to Brandon? The moneylender?" Ben asked. Her sympathy was sweet indeed, but he needed to know. If Burke had indeed sought justice for poor Pamela, then at least Ben could rest easy on her account.

"Well, I could look, but…I'd probably need the computer, instead of just my phone."

Reluctantly, she climbed out of his lap and seated herself before the screen. Fifteen minutes later, she had her answer.

"George Brandon, notorious London crime boss in Georgian and early Victorian times. He owned brothels and gaming hells from London to Brighton, and was said to be rich enough to buy all the royal holdings in Britain, or so he said to his debtors before he fleeced them for all they were worth. He claimed to be the bastard son of a prince and an earl's wife, though there was no evidence he had such parentage. He disappeared mysteriously in 1851, when a gruesomely dismembered headless corpse was found in his office above one of his many brothels. Some say the body was his, and that the whores had banded together to butcher him like Julius Caesar, for being such a tyrant. Others say he escaped to the Americas, where he was killed in a slave rebellion, by his own slaves."

Ben closed his eyes. So, either Burke killed him, or Brandon had died at the hand of a woman. Both fitting fates for the bastard. Maybe Luce Iblis had been right, and Pamela truly was at peace, in the sort of afterlife such a gentle lady deserved.

"What year did Burke Castle burn?" Ben

asked.

"Also 1851."

He dared to breathe again. William Burke had been a fool, but he'd loved his daughter enough to do the right thing in the end. His heart felt light as air. He wanted to fly. Or better yet…

He swung Rochelle into his arms and kissed her soundly. One thing led to another, and he soon had his head buried between her thighs, until she was dripping wet with need for him as she begged for more than just his tongue. But she did not beg for long – no, Rochelle meant to be mistress of her own pleasure, he found, as she rolled with him until she sat atop him, inching her way along his body until she met the hardness she sought. She gave a little moan of pleasure as she impaled herself on him, before she began to move. Ben could not resist the siren call of her body, especially not when she squeezed him like that, as he laboured long into the night, to give this woman he loved everything she asked for, and more.

FIFTY-THREE

Ben spent his days at school, and his nights were Rochelle's. He'd started work on the painting, holed up in a spacious section between the roof and ceiling in the school's administration building, and he began to hope she might like the finished result. If she did not, he would keep it for himself, and when he was alone, he might feast his eyes upon her, fist himself in his hand and…

Ugh. Not when he was holding a tube of paint. Now he'd need to buy more ultramarine.

If this was what Dunstan had felt for Cara, after tumbling with her just the once, no wonder he had been so miserable when she'd married another man. Another man she'd tumbled daily for months, mind you, squealing like a stuck pig all the while.

Now if Rochelle were to leave him for another man…a real man, not some monster made out of living stone, who could not set foot in daylight. A man who didn't have a century-old vendetta to pursue…

Ben shuddered at the thought.

"But he called me a fairy, sir!"

Fae were monsters for sure, though he hadn't heard of any here. Perhaps the creatures had followed the colonists from Scotland. But the boy sitting in the office below with the school counsellor looked as human as any of the other students.

Gradually, as the boy and his counsellor conversed, Ben began to understand the situation better. It was legal to be a molly now, not a crime, but there were those who still made mollies' lives miserable for liking men more than women.

Ben might not learn as much about the world as he might if he lurked above a classroom, but he learned plenty about the people of this time, and their troubles. For all the differences, some things still stayed the same.

When evening came, he strolled down High Street to the café. The café was empty, so instead of setting up in the corner where he'd spend the evening closer to strangers than he was to Rochelle, he marched up to the counter to greet her with a kiss.

"I'm happy to see you, too," she said. "Do you want me to make you a coffee or something before you start work?"

If he'd had any need of sustenance, he'd have eagerly accepted her offer. The smell of her coffee or any one of the cakes was enough to tempt him. So he pretended to stare at the menu on the counter for a moment before he shook his head. "I'm fine."

Then a strange picture caught his eye on the television screen behind the counter. Normally he never looked at it, as it wasn't visible from the table where he sat to work, but now he could see the strangest thing.

"What is that?" He pointed.

"Hmm?" Rochelle glanced over her shoulder. "Oh, that's the Mothman, dancing on the roof of the building over the road. We've been playing this video and the other one on repeat since I filmed them, seeing as they went viral and all. We're still offering a month's worth of free coffee to anyone who can capture another picture of the creature, but he only seems to come out when I'm around."

Ben watched the video. A winged man danced jerkily across the rooftop, before the video ended and the screen showed the footpath below. In the darkness under the veranda, a cloaked figure lurked. A woman ran into the figure's arms, before they both disappeared. Then the dancing man was back.

"Have you seen him?" Rochelle asked.

Actually, if he looked closely enough, it could have been him. The wings, the horns…except Ben had never in his life danced like that, and he certainly did not go around kidnapping women. Especially not with his wings out. Whoever these men were, or had been, they were foolish indeed to allow someone to photograph them so publicly. This world liked to hunt monsters, instead of sensibly avoiding them, like they'd been doing for centuries in Scotland.

"I have not, but I can tell you that he is no moth," Ben said. "That is a gargoyle. Two, if I am not mistaken, for the one on the roof is much thinner than the one on the footpath."

Rochelle laughed. "You mean those grotesque monster things they stick on the edge of churches, like drainpipes?"

Probably a good thing he hadn't told her he was one, then. Not if she'd only laugh at him, if she even believed him.

"Gargoyles have many purposes, the most important of which is protection," Ben said.

"Well, the girls who live there could probably do with a bit of protection. Maybe that's why they put that little gargoyle statue up on the roof."

"What?"

Rochelle led him over to the window, then pointed upward. "See that section of scrollwork, on top of the round pediment?

There's a little plinth up there, and on top of it is a fat little gargoyle with stubby wings. It doesn't look a thing like my Mothman, though."

Ben's eyes drifted down from the gargoyle statue, to the well-lit upstairs windows. The ones that had been dark the last time he looked at the building. "Someone's there," he said.

Rochelle shrugged. "Well, yes. There are two apartments above the shops. One of them is owned by a lovely lady who comes in for muffins all the time. I don't know who lives in the other one. Someone who doesn't like my coffee, I guess."

Could it be the butcher? Still there, after all this time? For only a truly evil person could possibly hate Rochelle's coffee or any of the café's offerings, which were all made with so much love.

Gargoyles guarded the building. Gargoyles just like him. The butcher wouldn't have left the guards behind if he wasn't still using the place, surely.

Tonight, once Rochelle had had her fill of

him, he'd sneak over the road and investigate. After all, it couldn't hurt to check, right?

FIFTY-FOUR

"Mmm," Rochelle sighed, curling up to his side. Ben would have given every cent he owned to roll her onto her back and bury himself back inside her until morning. Better yet, to never have to leave her at all.

But he owed a duty to his brothers' memory, and he could not delay that for his own selfish desires any longer.

Besides, if he left now, he might be able to return before dawn, to claim a kiss from the half-asleep lass before he departed for the day.

He slipped inside the walls of the new building, the limestone parting for him like water. Floor by floor, he searched, but he found no secrets. Well, he found two randy couples who were as wild in their lovemaking as himself and Rochelle, but he had no desire to waste time watching. If it was lovemaking he wanted, he knew where Rochelle waited.

It wasn't until he reached the cellars that he noticed something different. The stones here were older, not as smoothly cut. As though this cellar had been built long before the house above. Perhaps…

Down he went, gliding through concrete and flagstones until he found a second cellar beneath the first. A small chamber, this one, so filled with dust and cobwebs it was hard to see anything in the darkness. He stumbled about, banging into things, until he touched the stub of a candle, melted into a niche on the wall, alongside a box of matches. Within moments, he had light enough to see by, but he did not believe his eyes.

This was Pearse's secret cellar, exactly as he remembered it. Why, when he wiped away the cobwebs, he found the dusty lumps on the table to be the teapot and cups Pearse had used to drug them, and likely other unsuspecting men, if Rochelle had indeed seen two gargoyles just like him.

His brothers' bodies were gone, with no tracks in the dust to tell him where or how or even when they had been taken. Long ago, most likely, for the thick carpet of dust on the floor showed only Ben's own footprints.

But the boxes…the boxes that had glittered and almost glowed in the candlelight that night, filled with unimaginable riches, those were still here.

Hardly daring to breathe, Ben reached out to brush a century's worth of dust away from the nearest box. Gold glimmered beneath his hand, just as it had then.

Like a mad maid, he began to dust the room, clearing the dirt away to reveal a fortune beyond his wildest dreams. Than any sane man's wildest dreams.

Enough to buy a grand house where he and Rochelle might live, with enough left over that he might study art while she did whatever she wished, without ever having to make another coffee or listen to a man complain for half an hour about how a muffin had more or less nuts than the one beside it. He could pay someone to make coffee and muffins for her.

He pulled out a chair and half fell into it, his thoughts here, there and everywhere.

His brothers were not here. The gold was. Which meant the butcher could not be far.

But surely not close enough to stop Ben from taking a box of the stuff for himself. After all, the butcher had stolen it. Surely in all the years that had passed, people had given up looking for it. No one would appear to arrest him after all this time.

Then again…why had the butcher not touched any of it? Did he know of dangers that Ben did not? The internet was a wondrous thing, filled with more information than any man could understand. Perhaps today's police had not forgotten about the theft, and they could catch him faster than the ones who'd arrested him in his own time.

Then there were the gargoyles, too. They must be guarding the gold in the butcher's absence. Ben would take his chances against most men, but two gargoyles, as indestructible as himself? The odds would not be in his favour – the risk was too high.

Ben sighed. He dare not take any of the gold. Not yet, anyway.

He needed to find the butcher, and force him to turn Ben back into a man, so that he could be with Rochelle. No, he needed to find out how to make the change himself, so that he might transform not only himself, but the other gargoyles back into normal men. Then he needed to kill the butcher, as justice for his brothers. Then, and only then, could he claim the gold.

So that he might live free, and build a new life with Rochelle, if she would have him.

Ben blew out a breath. Yes. That's what he would do. He'd…

A scream rent the air on the street above.

He could feel Rochelle's panic.

Something was wrong.

Heedless of the gold or anything else in the secret cellar, Ben shot up to the surface.

FIFTY-FIVE

"How dare you cancel me! You're nobody!"

Ben expected to find Rochelle screaming, or at the very least, a woman, but instead it was a man throwing a monumental tantrum in the middle of the road. Well, a boy, really, for no self-respecting man would behave like a toddler, surely.

Oh, but it was Rochelle's former roommate. What was his name again? Jakob, that was it.

"Show yourself, Rochelle! I know you're in there, and if you won't come out, I'll have to come in and drag you out, back home where you belong!"

Ben shifted into the shadows, where the darkness might hide his true form. Horns, wings and all, for the moment he'd threatened Rochelle, he'd summoned the monster. A monster who would allow no one to hurt her, ever again.

Best he deal with this quickly, before Rochelle woke up and saw him. Or perhaps she'd just believe he was the Mothman she'd filmed in the past. Maybe she'd even film him dealing with Jakob, and post that upon her video channel, attracting a new horde of customers to the café to hunt the monster. A monster who would happily draw their likeness for a fee while they drank their coffee and waited for a glimpse of what they did not understand.

"What is it, Jakob? Is this about the restraining order?"

Too late. The upstairs window flew open, and it framed Rochelle, hastily wrapped in a robe to hide her nakedness.

"The court agreed to issue it this week, so I imagine if you've received it by now, you understand that you're not allowed to be this close to me, or the police will arrest you. Go home, Jakob." She raised her arms to close the window.

"Don't you walk away from me! You're nobody!" he screamed. "You can't cancel me like this! Cancelling my internet will not stop the signal! I will be heard, or my fans will destroy you!"

"I cancelled my internet. If you want internet access so much, you can pay for it. Goodbye, Jakob."

"You're just jealous! Jealous because I'm a successful star, and you're nobody! You're so useless at filming, even the university staff can see it! Failing every assignment, failing at life. You're just embarrassing yourself, trying to be me, when you'll never be good enough. Never!"

"Actually, I passed my last two assignments. I might end up getting my degree after all, no thanks to you."

"Everything you are is thanks to me! Everything! You're no one without me, and I'll show you! I'll show everyone!"

"Whatever, Jakob." Down came the

window, and Rochelle disappeared from view.

Ben took a step forward, out of the shadows. He intended to see this idiot as far away from Rochelle as possible. Perhaps he'd fly him out to sea and drop him in.

"What's the matter, son?" Two police officers appeared on the footpath, scant metres from Ben.

Ben ducked out of sight.

"That crazy bitch is trying to drive me out of my home, cancelling my show!" Jakob flailed an arm in the vague direction of Rochelle's window.

She'd closed the window, but Ben could still see her up there, pacing worriedly in the shadows. She might have sounded calm and dismissive, but she was anything but.

"Move along, son, you're causing a disturbance. If you don't move on, we'll be forced to arrest you, and we don't want that, do we?"

"It's her you should arrest! She's crazy! Stealing my home, my show, sullying my good name with trumped up charges that aren't true!" His voice rose to a shriek.

"Maybe that's so, but that's no reason to

make a fuss. We need to keep the peace, and you're definitely disturbing it. Last chance, son. Will you move along, or do we need to take your details and take you down to the station?"

It was the wrong thing to say. The idiot reared up, his voice rising up into a scream again. "Don't you know who I am? Don't you? I'm Jakob Tollak, Iago to my fans, and to them I am a god!"

The cops exchanged glances as one of them noted down Jakob's details. "Isn't that the guy who escaped from prison a few weeks back? The one we delivered a temporary restraining order to yesterday? Better bring him in. Especially if he's in violation of the order already."

To Ben's delight, they handcuffed Jakob and started to lead him back to the station.

"You'll be sorry! You can't cancel me! I'll go back to my parents' place and use their satellite link. I'll show everybody what a loser you are, what a failure you've always been, and you'll be sorry! You're nobody!"

FIFTY-SIX

"You're nobody!"

Jakob's shouts echoed around the room, even with the window shut. Rochelle fell to her knees, her eyes too blurred by tears to see any more.

He was right, of course. She was nobody.

Even Ben hadn't bothered to stay – he'd gotten what he came for, and left the moment she was asleep.

"Are you all right?"

The voice was Ben's, a deep purr that had

always made her feel better. Not tonight, though. Nothing could do that.

"Where were you?" When she'd wanted, no, needed him…

"I was outside, debating whether to knock that idiot on the head and bury him in an early grave, or to drag him back to his house and stick his head in the toilet, to give him a taste of his own shit."

Rochelle almost giggled at that. He couldn't be serious.

Ben moved closer. "I had hoped to get rid of him, one way or another, before he woke you up, but I failed spectacularly. The police stole my thunder, and I suspect he's going to be spending a very uncomfortable night in their cells, while you enjoy some well deserved peace and quiet."

"Probably for the best." She sighed. If she had any sense, or if she wasn't feeling like a wrung out dishrag right now, she'd summon the last of her courage and tell him to go home. Not to waste his time on someone like her. "I wouldn't have wanted you getting arrested for a nobody like me."

"You're not nobody."

It sounded sweet, and maybe he even believed it, but that didn't make it true.

"He's right. I am nobody. I'm a talentless nobody who's failed more university units than I've passed, to the point where they're probably going to kick me out and never let me graduate. Jakob has a successful video channel, with thousands of fans who watch every video he posts, and here I am, living in the attic above the coffee shop where I spend every day serving coffee and muffins, smiling until my face aches, at whingers who want to complain just to hear the sound of their own voice."

Ben's arms wrapped around her, and hauled her to her feet. "You're not nobody. You're Rochelle Bourke. You make the best coffee and muffins in Fremantle, and the whingers all come here because you're the best listener, with the most beautiful smile, and you're kind enough to actually listen instead of telling them to go away. You've taken a struggling café, and your viral marketing videos have turned it into a thriving business. In fact, your two Mothman videos have more views than every video on Jakob's channel combined."

Rochelle shook her head. "That's not true. He has fans. Actual fans, who watch every week. I just posted two short, blurry videos I took on my phone. They can't possibly…"

Ben pulled out his phone, and showed her. Thousands, and millions. There was a whole extra zero on the Shut Up channel than there was on Jakob's.

"Shit."

But just because more people liked the Mothman than Jakob's gaming videos didn't change anything.

"I'm still nobody."

"No, you're not. You're the sweetest, kindest, most beautiful woman I've ever met. You're so amazing in bed, you're all I can think about. All I can draw, since the moment I first kissed you. You're bewitching. One smile from you, and all I can think about is what I can do to make you smile again. Sure, maybe there are a lot of things you haven't done yet. You're young. You have time to do everything, then change your life and do everything again differently. You've made an ex-convict believe in happy ever after again. Because you can build a new life, no matter how bad things get. You're the mistress of your own destiny. You're also the woman I love."

Rochelle swallowed. Had he truly said that?

"You're the woman I love, and I think it's time I showed you how much I love you, until you forget any of this ever happened."

She managed a watery smile. "That's pretty hard."

He lifted her in his arms and carried her to the bed. "Well, pretty hard is my specialty, especially when I'm naked with you. What do you say to allowing me to worship your body like the goddess you are?"

She had to laugh at that. "What woman could say no to that?"

"Nobody," she thought she heard him say, but then his lips were on hers, and his hands were stroking her, and there was nobody else in the world who mattered but her and Ben.

FIFTY-SEVEN

When Ben arrived at the café the following evening, he was surprised to see Tacey at the counter and not Rochelle. "She's at the prison tonight," she reminded him.

Ah, yes, of course.

"I'm sure she'd love it if you joined one of her tours. Go on, take the night off. I'll tell anyone who asks for you that you'll be back tomorrow," Tacey urged.

If Ben didn't know better, he'd think Tacey was trying to matchmake him with Rochelle.

Little did she know that Rochelle already owned him, body and soul.

He bowed. "Thank you, I will."

But instead of heading up High Street, toward the prison, he crossed the road, to stand before the house whose shadows had hidden him last night. Below him was the butcher's gold, and somewhere, behind the windows that glowed with warmth, were the answers he sought.

He took to the walls, searching for the house's inhabitants. He found all of them in a dining room together, having dinner.

Ben burst out of the wall, spreading his wings wide so as to look as frightening as possible. "Where is William Pearse?" he roared.

The blonde woman shrugged. "Who?" She stabbed something with a fork and lifted it to her lips as if nothing was amiss.

"William Pearse, the butcher!"

The men rose slowly from their seats, as if they'd finally decided he was a threat. The one who'd been sitting next to the blonde sprouted wings, just like Ben's. "There's no one here by that name, so you'd best be on your way, friend."

Something warm and furry rubbed against Ben's ankle. He glanced down to find a small black cat twining herself with great determination around his legs. Purring, for heaven's sake.

"I will not leave until you tell me where William Pearse is! I have business with him that will not wait a moment longer!"

The dark haired girl pulled out her phone. "Well, I can look him up and see if he has a social media profile. Maybe you can message him. Now, how do you spell Pearse?"

This was not going at all how Ben had hoped. "Damn it, where is Pearse?"

That was surely one of Pearse's gargoyles, so he had to know where he was.

Yet it was the other man who spoke. "You know, I think I do remember a Pearse. I think he was a butcher. But it was so long ago…he's probably dead now." He twirled his fork into a mess of noodles, then lifted it to his mouth.

The gargoyle looked longingly at the other man's dinner. "Probably," he agreed.

"Mrow?" The creature had clawed its way up Ben's pants and now clung to his shirt, butting his hand.

"What is wrong with your cat?" he demanded, patting the creature.

The blonde woman blinked. "Oh, Lucky likes gargoyles. Like, really likes gargoyles. She'll follow you around the walls, waiting for you to pop out so she can rub up against you. I thought we had rats at first. Gargoyles are so much better." She laced her fingers with the gargoyle's, and squeezed, like they were a couple.

Ben sighed. So much for threatening them into giving him what he wanted. He tucked his wings away, and reshaped himself into the unassuming form Rochelle knew best.

The man's fork clattered to the floor. He jumped up from the table, his face whiter than the moon. "Ben?" he whispered. "We thought you were dead!"

The blonde woman stared at him avidly. "The prison records say you're dead, but evidently they made a mistake. Interesting." She sipped from her water glass.

The gargoyle folded his wings away and squinted at Ben. "Ben?"

Ben blinked. At first, he hadn't recognised them, but now he could see the two men, side by side, sans horns... "Tor? Dunstan? You're alive?"

The blonde woman rose, collecting the plates. "Right, I guess dinner's over, then. Get the brotherly reunion hugs out of the way, because we're going to go the lounge room next, where we're all going to sit down and you," she pointed at Ben, "are going to tell us everything. Or I'll set the cat on you."

Whoever she was, this was not a woman to cross.

"Yes, ma'am," Ben said.

"Anemone, please. I've only just broken your brother of his bad habit of calling me his lady all the time."

"Yes, ma'...Anemone."

She tried not to laugh. "You'll do."

FIFTY-EIGHT

"Only Pearse could have possibly completed the spell, and woken me up, so he has to be alive," Ben finished.

"I'm sorry, I have no idea," Anemone said. She turned her laptop so Ben could see the screen. "I've looked, but all I can find is that he disappeared about the same time as the records say you died. He certainly didn't wake Tor or Dunstan. That was Catena and I, or that's what we believed."

Nods all around.

"Then how did you break the curse, if Pearse didn't do it?" Ben asked Tor.

Both Tor and Catena turned red.

Tor coughed. "Well, we thought it was because we had sex, but…"

"That didn't work for us," Anemone said, rubbing her belly.

"So breaking the curse might be more complicated than we thought," Catena began, tearing her eyes away from Anemone. "My friend, Callie, says the only way to break the curse is to melt a heart of stone. She has an old spell book with a ritual we think might have been used to turn people into gargoyles. It certainly sounds like what you remember, Ben, so it makes sense that the rest of what it says is also true. Perhaps Callie might know more. There might be alternative translations that give us more information so that we can help you and Dunstan break the curse on both of you, too. I mean, I know the wings and horns are handy, but you have to miss sunlight."

"And food," Dunstan added.

"All right, so we should go see this Callie. But first, we should probably bring up the gold, because only gargoyles can get to it."

All four faces turned to stare at him. "What gold?"

Fifteen minutes later, he stood in the hidden cellar with Dunstan, each of them armed with Anemone's high-powered torches. Catena had offered her phone so Ben could take pictures, but he'd told her he had his own. At her look of disbelief, he'd been forced to pull it out and tell her he used it to access the internet, and so that clients could contact him during the day. She still hadn't looked convinced, but she was as eager to find out about this gold as the rest of them, so she let it go.

Dunstan stared around him in wonder, as if he'd never been in this room before.

"That's where he put your body." Ben pointed. "Tor was over there."

"I remember waking up in the dark, rising up through stone, and then...Anemone," Dunstan said slowly. "But I don't ever remember seeing this."

"What else do you remember?" Ben asked, curious.

Dunstan shrugged. "Not much of anything,

really, before I woke up. There's a faint memory of you, more your name than anything, and Cara, which is a whole world of hurt."

Ben nodded. "Well, you did tumble a pregnant woman who was engaged to marry another man. I don't know how you thought that could ever end well."

Dunstan just shook his head. "I don't remember any of that. I only remember her sending me away."

Most strange. Ben had no problems remembering everything, except the time he was asleep. What made Dunstan different?

"Did Tor lose his memories, too?" If he hadn't, then perhaps the butcher had botched the spell on Dunstan.

"Yes. He didn't remember a thing until he and Catena broke the curse, he said. He didn't even remember he had brothers. At least I remembered you." He sounded pretty proud of that.

"Maybe he stuffed up the spell on me, then," Ben mused. Actually, that could be true. The butcher hadn't finished the spell, so Ben had kept his memories, while his brothers had lost theirs, at least temporarily. Hopefully, Dunstan would remember things when they lifted the curse.

"Where's the gold?" Dunstan asked.

Ben used the brush Anemone had given him to sweep the dust away from one shelf after the other. "All in these boxes," he said.

Dunstan's eyes widened. "Wow."

Wow, indeed. Ben weighed one box in his hands, then began to count them. "I estimate there's a little over two hundred kilograms here." When Dunstan looked lost, Ben did a quick calculation in his head. "Maybe just under five hundred pounds?"

Dunstan nodded. "We should probably get Tor to help. It will go faster, then."

"To get Tor down here, we'd need to find a way in that doesn't involve walking through walls. There was a ladder over here somewhere…" Ben scanned the room, searching for the spot. Ah, there it was, but it was so caked in what appeared to be dried mud, he hadn't recognised it at first. He scaled the ladder, only to find the way blocked at the top. There had been a hinge here before to lift the false privy seat to allow them to climb up, but either the hinges had corroded in place or someone had nailed the whole thing shut.

There was nothing else for it. Ben bunched up his stone fist and punched his way through. He emerged into a closet of sorts…no, a privy, walled up so no one would find it. He battered his way through those boards, too, and found himself in a cellar full of more modern furniture than that down below, but far more battered than anything he'd seen in Anemone's apartment. But there was an electric light in here, and a door that led through to the entrance hall.

"You can come up, I think I've found the way out," he called down to Dunstan.

"It might be better if you came down. I think I've found the butcher you were looking for, and he's in a bad way."

After a quick examination of the body Dunstan had found, they returned to the others through the walls.

At the mention of a skeleton, Catena refused to let anyone go down there again. "If there's a body, we'll need to call the police."

Dunstan and Anemone looked worried. "I can't…" he began.

"Me neither," Ben said. When no one else said anything, he continued, "Look, we can wait a few days before we call them, can't we? I mean, as long as no one disturbs the cellar any more than we already have. I might be able to find somewhere that you can stay for a day or two while the police investigate. Both of you."

"Thank you," Anemone said. "I wish I could go and hide, too, but the police already know me, so it's probably best that I stay to field any difficult questions. Catena's about to start her PhD on hidden objects in houses, so we'll say you were looking around our house, doing a little investigation of your own, and found the hidden chamber. You looked around, found the body, and then called the police. As soon as we can find somewhere for you boys to stay."

"On it," Ben said. They all stared at him, as though he'd said something wrong. Perhaps they'd misheard him. "I said I'm on it."

Anemone smiled. "You're not like your brothers at all. Intriguing. All right then. Come visit again when you have an update for us, please."

He'd been dismissed.

That was fair. He'd interrupted their dinner, after all, before he'd busted a hole in their cellar. If he was them, he wouldn't invite him over for coffee and cake, either.

He wished his brothers and their lovers goodnight before he headed back out to the street.

FIFTY-NINE

The café was still open, and Tacey stood behind the counter, cleaning out the sandwich cabinets. Ben had expected Rochelle, but she was probably still at the prison. He should head over there so he could walk her home soon, but, in the meantime, Tacey might be able to help him.

"Can I ask a favour?"

Tacey looked up. "You can ask. But if you want a sandwich, go ahead – take your pick."

Ben shook his head. "I was wondering if

you know where the university is."

"Which one? There's five main ones, plus some satellite campuses dotted around the place."

"I don't know. Someone told me I need to go to the university to consult a Latin scholar named Callie."

Tacey burst out laughing. "Oh, that would be Notre Dame University, just around the corner. But there's no need for you to go there. Callie is my housemate. I'll ask her to come by the café one night when you're working. She was intrigued to hear we had an artist in residence at the café. I'm sure she'd love to meet you."

Ben thanked her, then checked the time. If he hurried, he'd get to the prison in time to walk Rochelle home. When he'd have to ask for an even bigger favour – if she knew somewhere he might be able to accommodate his brothers for a few days during the police investigation.

SIXTY

"One chai latte with coconut milk, and do you have any muffins or friands with coconut in them to go with it? I think Tacey does a couple of them with raspberry or butterscotch."

Rochelle looked up to find Callie at the counter. "You forgot the lamington one."

Callie laughed. "Who could forget Tacey's twist on lamingtons? But I know she only does those for special events like Australia Day, and they sell out pretty quick. At this time of the afternoon, I've got no chance."

"Well, it looks like there's one butterscotch muffin left, if you want it."

"Oh, hell yes."

Rochelle rang up the order, then began to make it.

"So, which one is your artist in residence?" Callie asked in a loud whisper.

Rochelle didn't need to look up to check. "Ben won't be here until after sunset. Something about the light. But when he does arrive, that table is reserved for him." She pointed to the corner where the wall was now covered in his sketches.

"Then that's where I'll sit to wait for him."

Rochelle had to swallow down the lump in her throat as Callie took Ben's usual seat, sipping her chai completely oblivious to the position she'd usurped. But she was Tacey's friend, and moreover Tacey's roommate, and Tacey would not be pleased if Callie complained about one of her employees being rude to her, like Rochelle wanted to be.

Then a large group of customers came in, all wanting complicated hot drinks to accompany heated-up muffins and brownies, topped with

Tacey's new brandy sauce and custard.

By the time she'd delivered their entire order, Ben and Callie were so deep in conversation, he barely noticed her.

She sighed. He'd been really quiet on the walk home last night, lost in thought, that she hadn't wanted to pry. Yet he'd just met Callie, and now he was talking as though they'd known each other forever.

Rochelle had never been a jealous person before, and she wasn't sure she was one now, but it hurt to think the one man she'd begun to care about didn't trust her enough to confide in her.

Maybe he'd tell her everything later. When they weren't in a crowded café full of people clamouring for more brandy sauce.

She sighed, collected up the empty cups, and took them back to the kitchen to make sure they were washed.

SIXTY-ONE

"I'm Callie." The pixie-like girl stuck her hand out, her eyes appearing huge beneath her cap of dark hair.

Ben shook her hand. He would never get used to this modern habit, no matter how many times he did it. "Ben Stone."

"The unusually handsome artist in residence at the Shut Up Café, and Rochelle's new ride, if the rumours are to be believed." She winked.

Ben had learned a lot of modern figures of speech, but this one eluded him. "I'm sorry, I don't understand," he said.

This only widened her smile. "Ooh, a gentleman! Goddess knows she deserves one, after that gaming arsehole. And she keeps looking over here, like she thinks I intend to steal you. Well, you make sure you tell her I wish you both the best together. But you didn't invite me here for my blessing, unless you wanted it done in Latin. Tacey said you were interested in gargoyles."

Ben nodded and leaned forward, so his words wouldn't carry to the rest of the café. "I was talking to Catena, and she mentioned you had some sort of spell book that said how to turn people into gargoyles."

Callie folded her hands on the table. "It also says how to summon demons, make a man perish of lust, and ward a house from evil spirits, but there's no evidence to prove any of these things are even possible, let alone that the instructions in this book would result in the desired outcome, even if it was. And if you even think of casting any of these spells on Rochelle, or anyone else I know, I must inform you that I know some particularly nasty curses and I will cast every single one of them on you." Emphasised with a sharp nod.

She was a witch, Ben guessed, and she was testing him, before sharing her knowledge.

"What kind of curses?" he asked.

"I will curse your phone so that all the text appears in Ancient Greek. I will curse your nostrils so that you will smell nothing but ammonia for a week. And I will poison the minds of any woman who thinks to bed you, so that they believe you are infected with a deadly strain of genital herpes."

Ben relaxed. None of her curses relied upon magic at all, though he didn't doubt she could perform them. He'd managed the ammonia one himself, and had no desire to do it again. "I wouldn't mind brushing up on my Ancient Greek. I did have a classical education, but I admit I have forgotten much of my Greek and Latin. But Catena told me you were fluent in both Latin and Viking runes."

Callie sighed. "You're an arcane history buff like Catena, aren't you? All right, I brought scans of the book, and my translations. They're all on my laptop. In the meantime, I'll give you the short version I gave Catena…"

It was not short, but it was fascinating. It also made Ben shudder, for it took a most peculiar kind of person to kill someone, then cut up their cooling corpse, perform a bizarre ritual and bury them, before building their home on top of the grave. This book Callie now possessed might once have belonged to the butcher, for surely there could not have been two such evil people in such a small colony.

Ben tapped the screen. "So what do you think this means? You've translated it as melting a heart of stone, and that's what Catena told me, but that's an alchemy term that refers to a transformation into something else, a complex process that is nowhere near as simple as melting."

Callie appeared impressed. "I've never met a man quite so interested in arcane history…well, who wasn't a complete nutter who believed magic and witchcraft and spells were real. There's still a few of them around."

Ben ducked his head. He wished he didn't believe spells were real, but he was living proof that this spell worked. Now, all he needed was to make it stop working and he could go back to believing the world made sense again. "It's just a hobby, and a purely theoretical discussion," he assured her. "But what do you think the writer meant by this? Catena said it was just about sex. That sex could melt a heart and undo the spell, but I don't agree. Surely it can't be so simple…"

Callie nodded. "I agree. I mean, we're talking love and lust, for a start. Sex is the objective of lust, while love is more about the heart. There are many kinds of love, not all of which involve sex. And for most people, sex isn't exactly transformative. Well, unless you're talking about the power of the magic pussy."

Ben felt his cheeks grow hot. "I…uh…no?" He hadn't known it was possible to enchant that part of a woman's anatomy, and while he couldn't deny that good sex might appear magical, surely it wasn't because…

"Yeah, it only happens in romance books, sadly. Not real life. Anyway, there could be any number of things that they considered transformational. Traditionally, only enemies are used as foundation sacrifices, so perhaps the transformation is more in the head than the heart, because you'd need to seriously change your thinking for the kind of paradigm shift that turns an enemy into a friend, or even a lover." She coughed. "Which brings us to sex again. You know, if you haven't done it with Rochelle yet, you should really do something about the unresolved romantic tension between the two of you, because I swear I can feel the heat from here, and she's not even looking at me. Whatever your secret is, just man up and tell her already, so you can get to the passionate sex part. She really looks like she needs…" Callie gulped, then pasted a big smile on her face. "Hi, Rochelle! Are you coming to the girls' night Tacey has planned for next week? It'll be at Alethia's place so as not to wake up Rory, like we did last time."

Rochelle shook her head. "I'll be working, either here or at the prison. You all have fun, though. Is there anything else I can get you? Another muffin, maybe?" She looked from Ben to Callie, but they both shook their heads. "All right, just let me know if you change your mind." She collected Callie's empty cup and plate and left.

"Please tell me you're not going to leave her hanging," Callie said.

Ben stiffened. "I assure you my attentions toward Rochelle are purely honourable."

"Yeah, yeah. She could do with a bit of honourable after the last bloke, but I'm just saying, you should make sure it comes with a big side order of dick. Good dick."

Ben wasn't sure what to say to that. In all his years, no one had every questioned the…goodness of his penis. Finally, he just nodded. That seemed to satisfy the strange woman.

"Well, what else did you want to know about foundation sacrifices? Except that they sound seriously gross and twisted, and anyone who does them has some serious issues?"

Like Pearse. Ben shuddered. "Yeah, cutting into bodies like that would take a decidedly twisted mind. I can understand why they'd choose to do it to their enemies. I couldn't imagine doing something like that to the bodies of your family or friends, or anyone you cared about."

Callie did not look pleased. "Please tell me you are not going to try to make a gargoyle, or I swear to you, I will make good on those curses, only I'll swap out the Greek for kanji and then you'll be sorry!"

Ben raised his hands in surrender. "I have no intention of sacrificing anyone. But I have seen…where it was done. Once. It was not pretty." It still wasn't, and he needed to find somewhere for his brothers to stay so the police might begin their investigation.

"Well, it's been fun, but it's my turn to cook tonight, so I should be going. Now, Mr Honourable, will you at least promise to kiss Rochelle tonight?"

He inclined his head. "That I will certainly promise."

SIXTY-TWO

The following day, ensconced in his secret art studio in the school ceiling, Ben couldn't seem to concentrate. All he could think about was how he could possibly be there.

From what he'd understood from Callie and her spell book, the ritual had involved giving them a combination of herbs in a drugged tea. Like a form of modern anaesthetic, he presumed, prior to surgery that was more like butchery, which is likely why Pearse had not had any qualms performing the ritual.

According to Callie's book, the witch (for want of a better word) cut out the sacrifice's heart, then replaced it with stone, thus turning them into a paranormal protector made of living stone. But in order for the sacrifice to be summoned later to actually perform his protection duties, his body had to be laid to rest beneath the land he was to protect, and a stone laid atop his grave. There, the sacrifice slumbered until they were called into service.

Summoning the sacrifice involved removing the stone on top of the grave, and actually calling for them to help.

His brothers, laid to rest in the secret cellar with a road and a building on top, were proper protectors, until the removal of the road above had awoken them. Catena's call for help had summoned Tor to her aid, and Anemone's desperate cry for assistance, some days later, had brought Dunstan out of hiding.

As gargoyles, neither man had much memory of their past. They knew only what it was to be a gargoyle, and this compelled them to serve their respective mistresses, or charges. Ben wasn't sure exactly how that part worked.

He, on the other hand, had drunk the tea and possibly had his heart cut out, or partially so. The butcher must have managed to get the stone into his chest, too, or he would simply have died of his wounds and that was that. The guards who'd found him in the road had thought he'd died of his wounds when they buried him.

Not knowing about the ritual, their main concern was seeing that he had a decent burial, even if it was in a pauper's grave. He'd had no stone laid above him, so the ritual had remained unfinished. Ben had been as good as dead.

But someone, somehow, had finished the ritual. They'd laid and removed the stone, leaving no trace of it when Ben reached the grassy surface of the school sports field. Nor had he seen any sign of his summoner, who surely should have been there.

Unless they'd somehow been driven away before Ben had dug his way out of the grave. No one called for help unless they actually needed it, so perhaps the summoner had been in such great need, such great fear, that waking

Ben had been a desperate act, too late to do much good, for mortal danger was already upon them.

Pearse the butcher was the most logical person. He'd performed the ritual in fear of his life, and theft of his gold, so it made sense that he would have summoned Ben to protect him. Unless the skeleton in the cellar truly was the butcher. In which case, he'd likely have fallen down the ladder after Ben kicked him in his desperation to escape, killing the man. Which would make Ben a killer, if only in self defence.

Yet another reason for him to avoid the police investigation of the cellar. He had no desire to go back to prison, and he did not fancy trying to explain to them how he'd managed to murder a man over a hundred years ago.

If the skeleton did belong to the butcher, then it would take some serious arcane power for him to finish the spell and wake Ben. For a ghost or a shade surely couldn't lift a stone large enough to cover a man's body.

If the butcher still lived, then he still possessed unusual magical powers, allowing him to prolong his life for so long. Well, if he'd been human in the first place. If there were gargoyles and creatures like Luce Iblis in the world, then it made sense that other monsters might be walking among them, capable of all manner of remarkable things. A man who could live forever could easily have strolled up to Ben's grave with a piece of stone, finished the ritual, and then summoned Ben as his protector.

But if he had…why now, and why had he disappeared, if he'd needed Ben so much?

Neither scenario made a lick of sense.

There was also a third option. The spell book had perhaps passed from Pearse to someone else, or he'd borrowed it in the first place and been forced to return it. The book's true owner, then, had to be a powerful witch, capable of completing the spell Pearse had not.

The first and most obvious candidate was Callie. She was, after all, the present owner of the spell book and she was capable of both understanding and translating it. Except…Callie did not believe in magic. He recognised her scepticism for it matched what his own beliefs had been before he'd become the victim of a spell. She was forthright, too, in her unflinching talk of sex – if she'd believed in magic, she would have said so. Also, she'd been horrified that he'd seen a foundation sacrifice, which meant she evidently had never seen such a thing, outside of her spell book's description of it.

The second candidate was Rochelle. Sweet and kind and everything his heart could want, but he'd also seen her pretend to be a convicted killer in the prison. Rochelle was a capable actress, capable of fooling even him if she so wished. She was also the person who'd benefited most from his awakening – he'd lost count of the number of times he'd acted as her protector, and even now, he still felt the strong urge to keep protecting her. Could it be the same as the compulsion his brothers had described?

Except…neither Catena or Anemone had actually cast the spell in the first place. They had both simply asked for help at the right moment, and his brothers had answered their call. Perhaps Rochelle had merely called to him at the precise moment the spell had been completed, stealing him from the butcher or the witch who wanted to use him for their own nefarious purposes.

Which meant the witch was likely still out there somewhere, and a danger to both him and Rochelle.

Ben shook his head, but it didn't help the roiling headache building at so many twisting possibilities.

The most sensible thing to do would be to forget the witch, and try to break the curse. Then they'd have no hold over him.

If only he knew how to melt or transmute a heart of stone.

Finding the mysterious witch or, if he still lived, the butcher sounded much easier. More satisfying, too.

Ben nodded to himself and returned to his painting. It would be ready for her within the week.

SIXTY-THREE

Was that her phone? Rochelle swore and tugged off her headphones. She was trying to finish editing her latest assignment and she had to get the timing just right for the beats of this rapid montage…yep, that was her phone, all right, and it was her father calling.

Finally. It had been weeks since she'd last heard from him. He must have finished mustering and returned to the homestead.

"Hi, Dad," she said, plugging her headphones into the charger. This would likely be a long call. "How'd the mustering go? Did you get enough hands to help?"

She'd helped out a few times when Mum was still alive, but between uni and Jakob, she hadn't been back since. Listening to her dad's stories about this year's muster was almost like going home.

Even with the borders closed, they had enough first-timers to make life interesting, and she was soon laughing and wishing she'd headed north when she left Jakob, instead of staying in Fremantle.

But that would have meant giving up on any chance of graduating, which she wouldn't do, not while there was still hope. Her grades from this semester would either dash those hopes or see them ride again for at least another semester.

When her father finally finished describing the jillaroo's response when she'd realised donkey showers weren't powered by an actual donkey at all, she knew it was her turn to tell him…far too much.

"How are things in Fremantle with Jakob? I got the strangest email…"

Ah, so that's what Jakob had meant about making her sorry for…whatever he'd been upset about the other night. His revenge had involved sending an email to her father, telling Dad she'd gone mad because of all the things she was no longer doing for him. He'd ended the rant with a melodramatic threat that, as he could no longer live with Dad's mad daughter, he'd moved back to his parents' house, and he hoped Rochelle would see sense as she struggled to pay the rent and the bills without him contributing. When she contacted Dad to ask for his help, Jakob implied, and not before, he might be willing to accept her apology for neglecting him, but only if Dad gave him guardianship and power of attorney over Rochelle in case she went mad again.

Rochelle wasn't sure whether to laugh or cry. She wished she could remember what she'd ever seen in Jakob, but maybe he'd always been a bit controlling and…crazy.

"Has he moved out?" Dad asked.

"I don't know. I hope so. I've been staying at Tacey's place for a few weeks after he hit me and I went to the police. The court approved a temporary restraining order, but the day they delivered it, he decided it didn't apply to him and actually came to the café to find me. The last time I saw him, he was shouting nonsense as the police hauled him away. I guess I could go around to the house and check to see if he's really gone…" It was Gran's house, but for the first time in her life, she didn't want to go anywhere near it. Not if Jakob was going to be there.

"Don't go alone. Take someone with you. A couple of sumo wrestlers at least. And if he's gone, I want you to change all the locks. Every single one. I'll send you some money for a locksmith…but don't go alone. Promise me, Rochelle!"

"I'll ask my friend Ben. He works at the café with me and sort of fills the role of bouncer in the evenings. He's not as big as a sumo wrestler, but he does scare Jakob, which is probably all I need."

"Good." A long pause. "Do I need to meet this Ben fellow? I could come down to Perth, now the restrictions have eased."

It would be lovely to see him, but she knew

he was needed on the station. There was always a heap of admin to do in the office after being away for weeks of mustering. "I'll be fine, Dad. There's no hurry. I'm really hoping Ben sticks around, and if he does, you'll have plenty of time to meet him."

She had a sudden longing to take Ben north, to show him the red dirt station country where she'd grown up. The space and the colours and the wildlife…the things he could paint up there.

If he stuck around, and didn't get bored with her and find someone else. He had said he loved her, and she had no reason not to believe him, but she was fast falling in love with him, too, and it would shatter her heart in a million pieces if…when…if he left her.

She'd only had to see how well he'd gotten along with Callie to know how easily he charmed women.

A quick call to Crystal and the other girl agreed to cover her shift that night, so all she had to do was wait for Ben to arrive and also agree, before they were out of there, headed up the hill to Gran's old house.

"What did you say or do to Crystal to make her stare daggers at you like that?" Rochelle asked as soon as the café door had shut behind them.

"I merely drew her as she made a cup of coffee, like I draw you most nights. However, Crystal has some unusual scars that made it into the picture, so when I left that night to walk you home from the prison, she tore it up. I found the pieces in the rubbish bin." Ben shrugged. "I'm sure she has quite an interesting story to tell, but only to someone she trusts, and only when she's ready to do so. Until then, she will probably continue to wear long sleeves."

Rochelle hadn't ever noticed that about Crystal before. "Huh. You're not like other guys, you know. Most men would just say that she's a bitch, or that she just doesn't like you. But most people wouldn't have noticed scars she's so good at hiding…I mean, I didn't even know."

Ben grinned. "Funny thing, that. Most people like me. They just can't help themselves. When someone doesn't, though…it's rarely anything to do with me."

Again, on any other man that kind of overweening self confidence would have come across as arrogance. From Ben, though, and knowing how down to earth he was…

Rochelle shook her head. "Callie certainly liked you."

Ben laughed ruefully. "Callie seemed more interested in talking about you and trying to matchmake us. She was most insistent that you needed some…ah…good dick, as she put it, and she believed I should be the one to give it to you."

Rochelle snorted. "As if Callie would know good if it danced naked in front of her. She has so many stories about disastrous dates, I'm not sure if she's ever dated a guy for longer than a week. She finds them on dating apps, because everyone at uni thinks she's a witch and she's threatened to curse most of the staff at one point or another. Oh, and her students, but only if they cheat or plagiarise or any of the things students aren't supposed to do anyway. That scares off most of the people who know her, which leaves her stuck with dating apps, and the array of bottom feeders who seem to be attracted to her on them."

"She did threaten to curse me in at least three…no, it was four different ways last night. Particularly if I didn't kiss you."

"That was…" Rochelle fought to find the right word. "Considerate of her?" No, that wasn't quite right.

"I thought it was interfering and vulgar, especially when she asked for details about our intimate moments together. I believe she took my silence on the matter to mean we had not shared any intimate moments, which is when she began insisting that we should do so. With a great deal of coarse language."

Rochelle hid her smile. It almost sounded like Ben didn't like Callie. "You could have told her to bugger off and mind her own business. That's what I did when she tried that on me."

"Ah. I did not think of that. I was attempting to remain polite, because I wanted her assistance on translating some Latin I wasn't quite sure about. She did translate it, in between the other things she said, but I'm still just as puzzled as before. I wish people would be clear, instead of using flowery language to hide what they really mean."

"You and me both. I'm all for plain talking. Instead of lying or making things up or just plain hiding the truth…" A tear trickled down her cheek, and she paused to swipe it away. A quick glance at Ben told her he was looking away, so he hadn't seen it. "Do you know what my father told me? He said Jakob had contacted him, to tell him I was mad, and not to believe a word I said because of it."

"Did your father believe him?"

"Of course not. Dad's not stupid. He told me to get down to the house and change all the locks. He also told me not to go alone." Rochelle stared at Ben. "It's like he thinks Jakob's dangerous, when he's all hot air, really. He was always such a coward at school. If there was even the slightest whisper of a fight, he'd be off running to the office so the teachers could intervene. That's what first made his gaming videos famous – he used to go in, aggravate a whole mob of bad guys and kite them all over the place, screeching in terror. And that wasn't even real people. I'm not sure he even knows how to throw a punch. He wouldn't actually hurt anyone. Not on purpose."

Ben just shook his head. "The prison you take tourists through used to house the worst criminals in Western Australia. While some of them were very bad men, the sort who planned their crimes or took great pleasure in them, most of them were there because of a mistake they made. A mistake that cost someone their life. A momentary lapse in judgement. You may not remember, but I do. I saw that boy swing. I saw Jakob's blow take you down and knock you out. Had you landed on the stone step instead of the decking, that one blow might have killed you. Perhaps it was an accident. Perhaps he might never have done such a thing again. A man might regret something so much he never does it again. But that boy came to your new residence, screaming in the streets about how he would have his revenge. He also contacted your father, trying to discredit you. Those are not the actions of an innocent man. They are the actions of a man who started as he means to continue, so drunk on his own power that he will not stop. Perhaps the first blow was not on purpose, but everything he has done since had only one purpose: to hurt you."

Ben was right. Dad knew it, too. It was just so hard to believe, it hurt. "But he was my friend."

Ben nodded. "He was. But people change. I heard a school counsellor say to a student this week that when people change, they are becoming the person they wish to be, the person they truly are. Expecting them to change back is like expecting time to run backward. I can never go back to the boy I was before I was arrested. I cannot change what happened. I can only hope the man I have become will not make the same mistakes again, so that one day I might be the man I am meant to be."

Slowly, Rochelle nodded, too. "That's…pretty deep. You haven't been smoking anything, have you? Or is the truth that you're really a thousand year old vampire, who only looks like a guy in your early twenties, and that's why you only come out after dark?" She laughed at the shock on his face. "Sorry, Ben, but I'm sure that's totally the plot of a vampire book I read when I was in high school." She trailed off as they reached the driveway.

No light shone out the windows, but that might be because all the blinds and curtains were shut. Gran had insisted all her window coverings should block out the light completely, to keep the heat out in summer. Jakob had always insisted on keeping them closed all the time, year round, because of the strange hours he kept, gaming day and night.

"Well, here goes nothing. The house is dark, so we could be lucky…" She reached out to slot the key in the lock.

SIXTY-FOUR

Inside the house, a stack of unopened envelopes littered the hall table. Rochelle picked one up, looking like she wanted to linger, but Ben knew that was a bad idea.

"Let's search the house and see if he's here, before you do that. He could be hiding here in the dark, waiting to ambush you." Ben doubted Jakob would have the cunning to do such a thing, but he would not risk Rochelle's safety on a foolish assumption. "Stay behind me, just in case."

Searching the small cottage didn't take long, and the garden was empty, too. The room where Jakob had kept his computer was empty, as was his half of the wardrobe. It appeared he truly had left.

Rochelle collected all the envelopes and carried them up to the garden wall, where she climbed up, just like the first night he'd seen her.

On this side of the wall, the climb was almost effortless, unlike the precipitous drop on the other side. No wonder she'd chosen it for her eyrie.

There was room enough for both of them, so Ben hoisted himself up onto the crumbling limestone, too. The view up here was almost as good as the one from the lookout. He should have brought a sketchpad.

But as he hadn't, he watched Rochelle instead. She tore open the letters one by one, scanning the contents before shrugging, then setting them down. Envelopes in one pile, letters in another. Until one letter made the colour drain from her face as her hands shook.

"What is it? Bad news?" Ben pressed.

Rochelle wet her lips. "Probably. I don't know. The Vice Chancellor of the university wants to see me in his office on Monday morning to discuss my enrolment status. I guess I didn't do as well on my last couple of assignments as I'd thought I did, and if I fail this unit, they'll kick me out. I didn't think they'd bother sending a letter. They'd just lock me out of enrolling in next semester's units, and that would be that. Now I need to meet with the VC and…I guess I'm a little scared."

"I wish I could come with you." If he was a normal man, he'd be able to. As a gargoyle…not a chance.

"Yeah, I wish you could, too. But, seeing as you're a vampire and all…" She shrugged. "I'll be fine. Maybe I'll cry a bit, so if my eyes are red when you see me Monday evening, I'm telling you now, I will definitely accept any and all hugs you have to offer."

"I'll bring a selection for you to choose from. And, I believe I will also be able to bring your finished painting."

Her eyes lit up. "Really? Oh, that's wonderful. Definitely something to look forward to. Um, as long as you cover it up, because if it's half as raunchy as what you drew on paper, I'm pretty sure it qualifies as not safe for work, on a whole lot of levels."

He bowed. "As you wish, of course."

SIXTY-FIVE

The locksmith dropped off the keys to the new locks the following day, along with the manual for the new alarm system. "You'll want to change the code on that to something more personal that you'll remember," he said.

Rochelle didn't want the alarm system at all, but her father had insisted, and seeing as he'd paid for it… "I will." It was the last on a long line of things she'd have to do, before she moved back into Gran's house. Not least of which was finding time to actually move all her stuff back. Tacey and the others had that girl's night this weekend, which meant she was working for most of it, and none of them would be free to help her, so the earliest she could move back was Monday night. She really wanted to ask Ben to come with her, partially to help, but mostly as moral support, in case Jakob turned up, but he was later than usual tonight.

The reason for his tardiness followed him in, half an hour later – two men who looked as grim-faced as he did. But the resemblance didn't end there. There was something in the way they walked…and the way they stared around the café as though they'd never been inside one before. Which made no sense, because the Shut Up Café was just like dozens of other cafés in Fremantle, and one of millions the world over. Even the espresso machine was older than she was.

"Rochelle, I need to beg you for a favour. Something's come up, and my brothers urgently need somewhere to stay for the weekend. My place is little more than an art studio, with nowhere for them to sleep, and I have private commissions to complete over the weekend. Seeing as your house is empty at the moment and you're staying here still, I was wondering if you'd be able to put them up for a few days. I can pay you, and I can vouch for them fixing, cleaning or replacing anything they touch, as necessary. Please, I beg you."

He really did look desperate. His brothers were…well, she saw the family resemblance, though one of them was as wide as a sumo wrestler. Ben was easily the handsomest of the three, though the one who wasn't a wrestler did have a roguish wink.

Rochelle closed her eyes. She'd let Jakob stay there, rent-free, for years, and he'd never paid for anything, let alone fixed or cleaned or replaced stuff. And if Jakob came back over the weekend, angry that she'd changed the locks, it would be nice to have two burly men capable of tossing him out on his ear and telling her about it, instead of letting him frighten the life out of her if she was home alone next week.

This was for Ben, the man who'd done countless favours for her every day she'd known him. He was even doing a painting for her, for goodness' sake.

"All right, but I plan to move back on Monday. If you'll all help me move my stuff on Monday night, I'll consider it a fair trade."

Ben seized her by the shoulders and delivered smacking kisses on both her cheeks. "You are the sweetest, kindest woman in the world. Dunstan, Torstan – this is Rochelle, your new landlady for the weekend."

Her breath caught in her throat. She'd heard those names before. Alarm bells clanged in her head. Something wasn't right. Surely they could stay in a hotel or the backpackers down the street…why did they need her place?

She waited for Ben's brothers to leave – which they did, after giving her a curt nod each in acknowledgement of the introduction – before she leaned over the counter and hissed, "What's going on? Are they doing something dangerous or illegal in my house? Is that why they can't go to a hotel?"

"Your house, and your honour, is as safe with them as it is with me, I swear to you. They just need…somewhere to hide for a few days. It's nothing illegal, I swear on my life."

"But there's something going on, isn't there? Why won't you tell me?" They were going to be staying in her house, for fuck's sake. She deserved to know what they were up to.

Ben closed his eyes. "Look, there's…I don't want you to panic, all right? But there might be a police investigation at the house across the road from the café in the next few days with forensics and that bright yellow tape and people asking a lot of questions. It would be best if…my brothers and me weren't around here for that. And…it might be best if you don't know any of the answers, if someone starts asking, if you know what I mean."

"Ebenezer Stone, if this is something illegal, we are over, you hear me? I might not care about your past, but I do care about your present and whether we have a future, and if you're tied up in drugs or worse, then so help me, there is no future for us."

Even if it broke her heart to say it, she would not budge on this. God, just as she was beginning to believe she was in love with Ben, too.

He grasped her hands. "I swear to you, anything the police find is old news, from long before you were born. My brothers had no hand in any of it. It's old family history, that should have been dealt with long ago, but it wasn't and now we need to be absent for a little while, until this blows over."

She wanted to believe him. God, the way his eyes peered into her soul, as if he wanted her to read the honesty in his own. But the ideas running through her head, suspicions, really, were impossible. They just could not be. There had to be a reasonable, logical explanation for this and…

"On Monday night, I'll be coming home to the cottage, and when I do, you're going to tell me everything. What you and your brothers are up to. What you're hiding from. And why a couple hundred years' worth of family history might bring the police to my café now. Because if you don't…" Her heart would shatter into a million pieces, and she might never trust another man again.

"When all this is over, and the police are

gone, I swear I will tell you everything," he said.

Oh, how she wanted to believe him. "You'd better."

Then more customers came in, and he had commissions to sketch, while she had coffee to make, so they were forced to drop the subject, but this would not be the end of it, Rochelle swore.

SIXTY-SIX

When the sun rose, Ben slumped down into a seat at the kitchen table beside his brothers. With all the blinds pulled down, so little light penetrated Rochelle's house that it was possible for even a gargoyle to spend a day there without turning to stone.

"Do you mean to offer for the coffee girl?" Dunstan asked. "Because you're far too young to consider settling down. Tor and me, we're older, but you're barely one and twenty. No house or job or trade to support a wife or family…perhaps you should look to attending art school, as you meant to back in Scotland. Tor's started up a stonework business, so perhaps he can hire you to help him for a while, and then with the money…"

Ben burst out laughing. The world had changed, but his brothers had not. "What do you think I've been doing all this time, while you two have been sneaking about in the walls of the homes of the women you fancy, spying on them in the shower and such? I've spent my days at art college. The cemetery where the guards buried my body is now the college sports grounds, for the students here learn much more than just art. The Civil Rights movement and psychology and chemistry and computers… and they now teach art in schools to anyone. This year alone, I've already attended more art classes here than in the rest of my life put together. And I sell more of my work in a night than I did in a year back home in Scotland. The world has changed and it's an amazing place. I don't need your money. I make more than enough of my own, living among the people of this time as one of them.

I even have my own phone and email address and everything." He pulled the phone out of his pocket and waved it at them, wondering if either of them knew just how much the device was capable of.

Tor frowned. "Is that the device that takes pictures and sends them out into the ether for everyone to see?"

Ben nodded. "It's one of them, yes."

"If you know so much, how do we break the curse, then?" Dunstan demanded.

Ben blew out a breath. After his discussions with Callie and a great deal of thought, he had a theory. "We each have to break the patterns that led us to be cursed, and return to the paths we were destined to follow, before all of this. The paths the Queen of the Kelpies foretold back home, the night Pamela died." He pointed at Tor. "You were a master stonemason, ready to come to this colony to build it into a beautiful city. The night the butcher turned us into gargoyles, you were broken in body and spirit, not even trusted to break stone, let alone build with it, but now I see the brother who stood before the Queen with me, all those years ago. You might think it was bedding the archaeologist, but I think it was more than that. You remembered who you were, and what you are capable of."

Tor looked thoughtful. He likely would for a long time, for he was not one to jump lightly into agreeing with anyone. But he would see it, Ben was sure of it.

Ben turned to Dunstan. "You came here, brokenhearted at Cara's betrayal, swearing never to trust a woman again. You even cursed Pamela's name for dying, so that we might be accused of her murder, though she was hardly culpable for the crime, any more than we were. You talk to me of marriage and children and responsibilities, but your advice is as wrong now as it was then. Then, you spent all your time apprenticed in the shipyard, before you went to sea. If you'd stayed, maybe you would have been the one to seduce Cara and get her with child, instead of that brute Oscar. She wept after every tumble with him, for he never thought of anything but his own pleasure, and she would have chosen you over him if she'd thought for a moment you were home to stay, but away you went, so she had no choice but to tie herself to him forever."

Dunstan's brows drew together. "You and Tor both love to lecture me about Cara and Oscar, but I never saw aught amiss with either of them until she married the man and cast me out! Neither of you have been in love as I have, so you cannot possibly understand what it is to have your heart so shattered, you will never put the pieces back together enough to love another as she truly deserves!"

"Horse piss!" Tor snapped. "You never truly loved Cara, for you never really knew her. Now, Mistress Anemone, I've seen how you look at her. It's no different to how you used to look at Cara, only Anemone is every bit as sweet as she appears. God's teeth, man, she's carrying your child!"

"Wait…gargoyles can sire children?" Good thing he and Rochelle had used those condom things, then. Damned uncomfortable and they smelled strange, but he'd use a box of them every night until they agreed they were ready for children. If Rochelle didn't see him off when she learned what he truly was…if only he could find a way to lift the curse before Monday…

Dunstan laid a heavy hand on Ben's shoulder. "I suppose you are a man now, so you should know that whenever you bed a woman, there is always the possibility of conceiving a child. You see, your seed…"

Ben shoved Dunstan's hand away. "Don't bother, brother. I'd wager every penny I've made selling my art in this time that there's nothing you can tell me about sex that I don't know already, and that if I shared even a tenth of what I know about sex between a man and a woman with the two of you, both Catena and Anemone will tie you to their beds and not let you leave their bedchamber ever again." That wasn't even including other kinds of couplings, which Ben had seen but never tried.

Dunstan folded his arms across his chest. "If you know so much, then, little brother, tell me this: how do I break the curse?"

Ben thought hard. "I think that in the end, it will be up to you, but I'm sure you will need to let go of your bitterness about Cara, forgive yourself for the mistakes you make then, and resolve to do better as a husband to Anemone and father to whatever children she might bear you. But in order for the curse to break, you will have to make sure all of this is in keeping with the lady's desires, too, which I cannot begin to know."

Dunstan grunted, but he didn't appear to want to argue. "And what of you, then?"

Ben sighed and spread his hands out on the table. "I don't know. Unlike the two of you, I've never truly left the Queen's path. I am here, working on my art and headed for happiness. I may have strayed a little, in the pursuit of vengeance first for what I thought was the death of my brothers, and secondly for Pamela's murder, but…fate has had things all her way, as usual. Brandon died horribly at the hand of Burke himself, before Burke took his own life, I have since discovered. Fitting justice for them both. Pearse…if that is his body in the secret cellar, then he met his end at the bottom of a privy, buried beneath a pile of shit beside the stolen gold he never got to enjoy. Justice, surely, and at my hand, or perhaps my foot, as it was I who kicked him and knocked him off the ladder.

"I am an artist, like I always wanted to be, and if my patron is an ordinary woman who owns a café instead of some rich lord, then fate is smiling on me for once, because Tacey has never once made me feel inferior, for my presence in her café benefits her business as much as mine. I do not know what else there is left for me to do."

Tor straightened. "The Queen spoke of an heiress, and gold. Perhaps you need these in order to break the curse."

Ben shrugged. "We already found the gold, right there in the secret cellar. The police will likely return it to the rightful owner. Perhaps the Queen believed I would take it for my own, or that we would share it between us, and I admit I considered it, but it is so much harder to hide things in this time of computers and cameras and an internet that links the world in a blink of an eye.

"As for an heiress…perhaps she spoke of Pamela, and how I would make peace with Pamela's ghost, for the only woman I see in my future is Rochelle, if she will have me, and she is just a poor student, making coffee and working at the prison in every spare moment. Or maybe fate has more twists in store for me, as she usually does. Maybe Rochelle will reject me, and I have yet to meet this heiress, so I will remain cursed for some time longer, while I watch my brothers seek happiness with the women of their heart."

Both his brothers reached for Ben and each patted a shoulder.

"You'll always be welcome with one of us, little brother," Tor said.

Dunstan nodded. "Anemone has bedchambers for guests that no one ever sleeps in but her cat, and the cat will be most upset if I break the curse and she no longer has a gargoyle to curl up to. You may entertain her cat while she and I are otherwise occupied in her bedchamber. She likes neck scratches, but you are not permitted to touch her belly."

Ben wasn't sure if he was referring to Anemone or her cat, but he would heed the warning all the same, and avoid touching the belly of either female.

SIXTY-SEVEN

Between working extra shifts all weekend, and not seeing Ben at all since the night he'd come in with his brothers, by Monday, Rochelle just wanted to burrow back under the covers and hide from the world. But she knew she couldn't. She had to attend that meeting with the Vice Chancellor, in case there was any way she could beg him for one more chance to let her keep studying for another semester. Sure, the chances he'd agree were slim to none, but if she didn't go, she'd be kicked out for sure.

So she squeezed into the one business suit she owned, which she hadn't worn since her disastrous office internship last year. She'd known before the internship that she wasn't cut out to work for some big corporate firm, with marketing budgets the size of a small country's GDP, but whose idea of something fresh was an ad they'd seen last century for a product that had tanked then and wasn't likely to have a comeback any time soon.

No, she'd done her best work for Tacey's café, actually, or some of the short films she'd helped produce and promote when she'd first started university. Before Mum had died and her luck had gone sour.

When her film projects had started to go missing the year Mum died, the university had sympathised with her loss and given her plenty of leeway on deadlines and the quality of her work. But that time was over, though her luck hadn't changed much for the better. With the exception of the last month or so, she honestly didn't think it could have gotten much worse, even if things were about to now.

Rochelle sighed. Well, at least she still had a

job – two, if you counted the prison – and somewhere to live, even if getting kicked out of uni lost her Gran's cottage. She'd have to look for a new place to live, or she'd have to move back up north to the cattle station.

Something to worry about after her shift, and after this meeting.

Rochelle took a deep breath. "Hi, I'm Rochelle Bourke. I have a meeting with the Vice Chancellor," she said to the elegantly dressed receptionist who guarded access to the plush offices beyond.

The woman's eyes widened. "Oh, Miss Bourke. Yes, he said to show you right through. Such a terrible, terrible thing to happen, and all over the news, too."

Rochelle gulped. She'd been too busy to even check the news for days, and watching the police set up their marquees and caution tape over the road, just as Ben had predicted, had sent her scurrying away from any mention of what they were investigating. When customers asked about it, she'd just shrugged and told them she had no idea.

Because the ideas she did have alternated

between terrible, impossible, and otherwise unbelievable.

She'd been bagging up a muffin for Anemone when she glimpsed the police helping to load a body bag into the back of an ambulance. Anemone had noticed her preoccupation, glanced at the ambulance, then said, "I know. My neighbour Catena almost had a heart attack when she first found it. Who'd have believed it was buried in my basement all those years? I've been rushing out early and coming home late, so I don't accidentally see what else they find down there."

"Miss Bourke?"

Rochelle blinked, dragging her thoughts back to the present. "Oh, yes, terrible," she murmured, hoping that was the right response.

"Right through the door over there." The receptionist pointed.

Rochelle tapped timidly on it, until the man sitting at the desk looked up. "Yes?"

"I'm Rochelle Bourke," she said.

His eyes widened. "Oh. Thank you so much for coming. If you would please close the door?"

Well, it was probably best the receptionist didn't hear her beg to be allowed another chance. She was going to see her run out in tears, anyway, which was bad enough.

"Please take a seat, Miss Bourke."

Yes, because if she gripped the arms of the chair tightly enough, she'd be able to stop her hands from shaking.

The Vice Chancellor steepled his hands together, then took a deep breath. "I wish to assure you, that nothing like this has ever happened in the almost thirty years since this university first opened. That it has happened at all has shocked every member of staff here. To have it brought to our attention by the media, instead of coming through official channels, where the matter might be handled discreetly to the satisfaction of all parties…well, it's too late for that now." He regarded her with something that looked like disappointment.

Her heart sank. Too late. "I understand," she said, though she didn't. What was she supposed to have done – come in to beg earlier, instead of actually working on her assignments and trying to achieve good enough results? She didn't want to get better results from whining – she wanted to be judged on her merits. To know she was good enough to graduate and do what her degree had trained her for.

But it was too late, and if she stayed here a moment longer with him judging her for her failure, she was going to cry and she wasn't sure she'd ever stop. Rochelle jumped to her feet. "Thank you for your time, sir."

"Please sit down, Miss Bourke. I beg you. Just because the university has allowed this to happen does not mean it cannot be set right, however late it might be. I still hold out hope that we can reach a mutually beneficial outcome, without further negative media. As a student of commerce, and communications and media, I'm sure you understand more than anyone that it is the outcome, and the message conveyed by it, that matters more than what might have happened."

A student who would never graduate, unless he was offering her the chance to continue…for even this faint hope, Rochelle was willing to do as she was told. At least the chair was comfortable.

"What do you propose?" The words were calm and composed, sounding so professional Rochelle could hardly believe they'd come out of her lips. But if the Vice Chancellor was offering her something, she'd be an idiot to refuse. At least until she knew what he was asking in return.

"First, for his blatant disregard of the university's code of conduct, Mr Tollak will be stripped of his degree and denied enrolment or credit for any of his studies at any university in Australia."

Jakob? This wasn't about her own failures, but something Jakob had done? Something so bad they'd actually strip him of his degree? That had to be serious cheating or plagiarism or…something like that.

"Just so we're on the same page here, can you tell me exactly which parts of the code of conduct Jakob violated to deserve this?" Rochelle asked.

The Vice Chancellor coughed. "Well, it appears he stole your work and submitted it under his own name for most of his degree, while your records show you requested an extension due to your assignment files being lost due to computing or technical errors. Clearly, this is blatant cheating and plagiarism of the worst kind. If you had submitted the assignments you had originally completed, it would have been obvious to the lecturers and the matter would have been dealt with, but because you never submitted them, it went unnoticed."

Hang on...Jakob had done what? "So you're trying to pin this on me? Say it's my fault Jakob was a lying, cheating, stealing..." She shouldn't swear, she really shouldn't, but there were no nice words for what Jakob was, so she settled on, "...douche bag?"

The Vice Chancellor winced. "Not at all, Miss Bourke. You merely asked me the extent of his violations, and I have told you. This does not begin to make up for the consequences to you from his theft, or from his actions after he obtained his degree. This whole mess started when Mr Tollak admitted on his rather public video channel that he has been stealing your assignments from your cloud drive, stating that he had done so in order to save academic staff from being subjected to the low standard of your work, before proceeding to publicly post examples of these assignments, which bear a startlingly close resemblance to his own submitted work. Several of your tutors brought the matter to the relevant unit coordinators, by which time the media had caught on to the possible scandal this might embroil the university in, and they contacted our public relations office for a statement." He smiled thinly. "I'm sure you can imagine what our statement was."

"That the university will conduct a full investigation into this matter, and will issue a media statement when there is something further to report," Rochelle said. She'd had to repeat the unit on public relations twice, thanks to Jakob, if the Vice Chancellor was to be believed.

"Precisely. I see why the staff and students at this university hold you in such high regard, Miss Bourke, and were willing to champion you in this matter. I believe there were even rumours of the university being cursed, if we did not act."

Callie. That had to be Callie. Rochelle would have to hug her when she saw her next.

"Over the last few days, we have conducted a full investigation, and the outcome put forward by your advocates on the academic staff might surprise you."

Rochelle crossed all her fingers. Hell, she even tried to cross her toes inside her shoes. If he was about to tell her she could stay on next semester and not get kicked out…

"Based on the reassessment of your unsubmitted work, due to theft, it appears that you have not only achieved sufficient credit points to be awarded a Bachelor of Media and Communications and, pending your grades from this semester, which I understand are not yet final but I have on good authority are sufficient to ensure you will pass all your units…it is likely that you will also meet the requirements to graduate with a Bachelor of Commerce in Advertising and Marketing, too. May I be the first to congratulate you on achieving a double degree?" He rose and offered her his hand.

Rochelle didn't take it. "At what price?"

For everything had a price, and two university degrees did not come cheap. He hadn't offered to waive her fees for them, after all.

"Why, preventing future unpleasantness, of course. The PR office has prepared a media statement, and they would like to include a quote from you about how happy you are about the outcome. We would also like assurances that you will make no further statement to the media, beyond the written one we will issue."

Ah, the price was her silence.

Part of her didn't want to be silent. If this could happen to her, it could happen to anyone. She hadn't seen it…what if making all this public helped someone else? Then again…Jakob had made things plenty public, and if she gave any interviews, she was bound to admit she'd had no idea about any of this until now. She'd look a right idiot for not realising Jakob had been sabotaging her all along, not some mysterious hacker or a simple computer fault.

So much for a degree earned on merit. Then again…

"Did the unit coordinators really assess all my assignments? Even the ones I didn't submit?"

The Vice Chancellor nodded. "Mr Tollak made every single one of them public, so they could see the ones he submitted were exact copies of yours, with only the names changed. He was awarded a number of high distinctions for your work, Miss Bourke. Enough to earn his degree easily, with an enviable grade point average, too."

Her GPA, not his. Or at least it would be, if she agreed to this.

"The offer is a limited one, as I'm sure you understand, Miss Bourke. Once you leave this room, the offer is no longer on the table." He ducked his head. "For what it's worth, I do believe you should take it. You have earned both degrees, no question. My offer is no more and no less than you deserve. I only wish we were in a position to offer you more. I mean, with your new, stellar grade point average, you would have a very good chance applying for an honours year in either of your chosen disciplines."

Research and academia…no, she had no desire to go there. Not even to be a lecturer like Callie.

Rochelle rose to her feet once more. "If I accept your offer, when will the graduation ceremony be?"

"In July, I believe. You'd have to check the university website for the date. I know it's in my calendar, as I have to be there, but I have a lot of appointments, so things can get lost in there sometimes." He paused. "So, am I to understand that you are accepting the university's offer?"

This time she shook his hand. "Yes. And you can tell your PR office or whoever's preparing the media release that I thank the university staff for your quick resolution of this matter, and I'm delighted at the outcome."

She might not be so delighted once she'd seen and heard what Jakob had said to make it happen, but that could wait until she got home. Right now, she felt like her luck had definitely changed.

SIXTY-EIGHT

Monday at the café was surprisingly quiet, allowing Rochelle to have the place packed up for closing exactly on seven that evening. As all her things still only fitted in one suitcase, she took a taxi up to the cottage, without bothering to call Ben or his brothers for help. Not that she had any of their numbers — something she needed to fix, if she intended to continue seeing Ben.

God, that was the question, wasn't it? She'd been just about walking on air when she left the Vice Chancellor's office, and a quick call to her father to tell him the good news and invite him down to Perth for her graduation had done nothing to dim her spirits, but now she remembered the plethora of police investigating Anemone's basement, and Ben's promised explanations.

She took a deep breath and blew it out. There had to be a perfectly logical explanation for all of this, which he would surely tell her soon enough. The crazy ideas flying through her head would simmer down or disappear entirely, and she'd be able to introduce Ben to her father as her new boyfriend at her graduation. Better yet, tonight she could celebrate the good news with Ben.

Yes. Focus only on the best case scenario and not…all the other things that could happen.

The key turned smoothly in the lock, a nice change after the incessant jiggling and swearing she'd had to do with Gran's locks. Rochelle rolled her suitcase into the entry and bumped the door shut again with her backside. The gloom engulfed her.

Had Ben and his brothers gone to bed already? Or maybe they'd gone out. Or maybe…

"Here, let me help you with that." Ben was there, in the sudden glow from the hastily switched on hall light, taking her suitcase from her. "Where do you want it?"

"In the bedroom."

He wheeled it away, without even pausing to kiss her.

This did not bode well.

She'd brought some food – mostly leftovers from the café – so she headed to the kitchen to put everything away.

Jakob, or Ben's brothers, had evidently cleaned the fridge out of whatever food she'd left when she decamped to the studio above the café. Even the ice trays in the freezer were empty, though some kind soul had left the empty trays there, perhaps in the hope that they'd magically fill themselves.

At least there was still tea left in the tin. Jakob wouldn't have touched it, and while Ben's brothers might drink tea, they evidently hadn't found hers. She set the kettle on to boil, then turned to find Ben seated at the table, looking like a man about to be led to the gallows.

"Before we begin this interrogation, may I ask you a few questions?" Ben said. "I promise they will not be too personal."

She shrugged. "You can ask."

"On the nights you sat up on the wall behind your house, did you ever see any weird rituals being performed on the sports ground at night?"

That definitely wasn't a question she'd expected. "What, you mean like witchcraft or satanic rituals on the school oval? No, why?"

"Well, it used to be a cemetery before it was a school, and a cemetery is the sort of place people might do that sort of thing. I figured if they had been, you might have noticed."

Rochelle shuddered. "Seriously? There's a cemetery behind this house? Underneath the school oval? That's just...ugh. I'm never going to have a good night's sleep here again."

"The gravestones have been moved to the new cemetery, but the bodies remain, I'm afraid. At least, most of them do. Did you ever hear or see anything strange there?"

He really wanted to know. Rochelle thought hard, but she had to shake her head. "Believe me, if I'd known about the cemetery, or seen anything like that…I probably would have thrown rocks at them until they went away. Especially if Jakob had pissed me off that night, which was pretty much every night toward the end."

Ben nodded for a moment, before his eyes widened as if he'd just had a sudden thought. "What sort of stones, and how far can you throw them?"

"Small chunks of limestone that have chipped off the wall, or were leftover from building the house. None bigger than my fist. And I don't usually throw them at people, but I might if I thought they were up to something nefarious."

"How far?" he pressed. This really mattered to him.

"Usually, just across the road. On nights when it rains, the whole road turns into a lake, and I skim stones across it. When I'm really pissed off, I just lob them as far as I can, over the road and the wall on the other side, and right onto the oval. Not when anyone's using it, obviously, but late at night, when no one's there…I was angry, all right?"

"So, it's possible that you threw a stone from atop your wall here and it landed on one of the old graves, then bounced off into the grass, leaving no trace of its passage except perhaps to complete a spell on the poor soul buried beneath…" Ben mused.

Rochelle had to laugh. "Well, it's possible if you believe in magic and spells and such things. I certainly don't. I mean, I might have filmed the Mothman, but even I know he's just a guy in a suit."

Ben sighed. "Then what I'm about to tell you might be difficult to believe, but I swear to you, on my life and yours, that it is the truth. And the fact that I am here at all, sitting at your kitchen table, talking to you, is because I am the monster you made me, accidental though your actions might be."

"Ben…"

"When I was sixteen, my brother and I were engaged to build a castle…"

SIXTY-NINE

"So the Mothman you filmed is not one man, but two, and neither of them was wearing a suit, or anything at all," Ben finished.

Rochelle's mind was whirling far too fast for her to catch up. She'd gone from the possibility of being kicked out of uni and becoming homeless to graduating and a homeowner and now her boyfriend thought he was a monster? Not just the sociopath kind, but an actual paranormal creature. It was too much.

"Please, say something," Ben begged.

She wasn't sure what to say, but then the words sort of spilled out of her and she couldn't seem to stop them. "You and your brothers came here in 1852 as convicts, convicted…"

"Wrongly convicted," he chimed in.

"Right, wrongly convicted of the murder of Miss Pamela Burke, the girl whose statue I saw in Scotland, which you carved while you were building her father's castle…"

"A folly. A castle ruin folly."

"A fake ruin, that now sits beside the real ruin that I visited…and you came here, built the prison and a bunch of other things, before you escaped with the help of a butcher, who turned out to be an evil butcher who put a spell on you…"

"On all three of us, but I woke up and fought back, so he didn't finish casting the curse on me and the guards found me in the street and buried me in the cemetery instead, where you woke me with a fortuitously thrown rock…"

Rochelle sighed. "So thanks to me and this

evil butcher, you and your brothers were turned into gargoyles who woke up in the present day as protectors. You can't go out in daylight, or you turn to stone, you don't eat or drink, which is why you've been pouring all the coffees I make you into the pot plants, and you hole up all day in the attic of the art college behind my house, painting commissions that you sell in the café where I work at night. Ben, you know this sounds crazy, right?"

"You filmed the Moth Men! You've seen them!"

At Rochelle's raised eyebrows, he continued, "My brothers! Tor, the one who vanished by taking that girl inside the wall, and Dunstan, who danced on the roof."

"Wait, you can walk through walls?"

He frowned. "Did I not tell you that? How do you think I left the café every morning before dawn, without leaving the door unlocked?"

She hadn't really thought about it, but evidently she should have. "I don't know, but I didn't think you were walking through the bloody walls!" Like a ghost. Like a dead man.

Which is what he was, or should be, if he'd been born in 1834, like he'd said. She buried her face in her hands. This was too much.

"At least let me give you the painting."

The painting of them together, having wild, glorious sex in front of the mirror. When he'd looked dark and mysterious and like he wanted to devour her. She opened her eyes and there it was, the most erotic picture she'd ever seen. One look melted right through her underwear and possibly the chair she was sitting on, too. She could almost feel him inside her again, driving her toward orgasm after orgasm as she screamed his name. The best sex of her life.

And then he put another painting on the table. Almost the same as the first, except for him.

In the second painting, he had horns. And wings. And was that a tail?

"This is what you saw. What you wanted. But this was the monster who possessed you that night, not caring a whit for anything but his own pleasure. This is my picture, my memory of that night." He held them up, side by side for a moment, before pushing the one with the man across the table to her, and hugging the monster to his own chest. "Forgive me, for you gave me the best night of my miserable life, though I do not deserve it, nor any of the nights you gave me after it, especially when I was supposed to be your protector. I fell in love with you that night, and I forgot who and what I was, and I did…the unforgivable."

She studied both pictures, comparing one to the other. There were slight differences, as you'd expect from two hand painted canvases, but it was the similarities that struck her. She was exactly the same in both, her head resting on his shoulder as she cried out in ecstasy. And the man, for with a dick like that he was every inch a man, was built exactly the same. Every muscle outlined in glorious detail in the mirror, though the massive, leathery wings framed the foreground of the monster picture. He looked like a demon, but he was still…Ben. She reached out to touch the wings, as if by stroking the canvas she might know what the monster's wings felt like.

Rochelle shook her head. This was silly.

Either this was his visual representation of how he saw himself, or he truly believed he was this monster, and he needed professional help.

"Show me," she said. "Show me the monster."

Ben nodded, then rose from his seat. Slowly, he stripped off his shirt, followed by everything else, leaving a neat little pile of clothes on the chair. When he stood there, as gloriously naked as the man in her painting, he asked, "Are you sure?"

Rochelle closed her eyes. Now she had a hot naked man in her kitchen, a man who claimed to be her protector. If he stood there naked much longer, she was going to climb him like a tree whether he was a monster or not. "Ben."

"Before I show you, I want you to know I'm doing everything I can to break the curse. My brother Torstan's managed it, and Dunstan and I have spent all weekend trying to work out how to be human again. We will work it out, I promise."

She fixed her gaze on him. "Show me the monster, Ben."

One moment she was staring at him. Then…she wasn't, and yet she was. Because he had wings.

"Whoa."

Horns and wings and a tail and…

"Are those ridges on your cock?"

She stepped forward to wrap her hand around it, just to be sure.

"All those times we did it with you like a normal man, when you could have been giving me this?"

He grinned. "Actually, I did. You just thought it was the condom."

Ohmygod. She'd been having the best sex of her life with a monster who had a magic cock and he was Ben.

Her mouth was dry. Her brain was screaming at her that none of this was possible, but her hands were telling her otherwise. His horns were rough and sharp. His wings were soft as well-worn leather. His tail swished as sinuously as any snake, before it circled her waist and pulled her closer, a steel band she could not escape.

Not even if she wanted to.

His chest was hot and hard with muscle, just the same as the man.

And his cock…rock hard and ready for her.

"I want that," she said, pointing at the monster picture.

"My painting?"

That, too. But first, she wanted to feel it for herself.

"Wild sex with a monster in front of the mirror. With you."

"But what if I hurt you?"

"You won't."

She'd never been more certain of anything in her life.

She led him to the bathroom, struggling to shed her clothes one-handed along the way. When the last scrap of fabric was gone, she pressed her hands against the mirror, pushing her butt against his groin. "I want you."

"And I want you, but I'm a monster, Rochelle. Now do you believe me?"

Yes, and no. He was still Ben and…

"I know that I want you."

Ohmygodohmygod THAT COCK!

Spearing deep inside her, rubbing against

her most sensitive spots until he filled her. Hard and fast, just like before. Only this time, it seemed like only seconds before the first explosive orgasm blew her away.

When her vision cleared, he'd twined his tail around her waist, pinning his hips to hers. His clawed hands cupped her breasts. "Now do you believe I'm a monster, Rochelle?"

She clenched down hard on that wondrous dick, making them both gasp, before she grinned. "You're my monster, and I love you, and I want you to do that again, but this time, don't stop."

Much, much later, when her wobbly legs refused to hold her up any more, Ben carried her to bed, wrapping her up in his arms and his wings, and she'd never felt so well-protected, or so loved.

When she awoke in the pre-dawn light, she was still in his arms, though the wings and other monstrous appendages were gone. All except for his monster cock, because that was hardly a curse at all.

SEVENTY

Several weeks later, Ben and Rochelle accepted an invitation to dinner at Anemone's house. It was just Ben, his two brothers, and Anemone and Catena, the girl who owned the other flat in the building where Anemone lived. When Rochelle said Catena looked vaguely familiar, Catena had just laughed and said no one ever noticed the university librarians.

Anemone served the pasta, setting out six plates of food as if she already knew.

"Did you tell her?" Rochelle asked, but Ben

shook his head. Only Rochelle knew about his new-found ability to walk in sunlight, which had come with the loss of his wings, and the ability to walk through walls. He'd had to buy new painting materials, as he couldn't return to his secret studio in the college ceiling after that first night he'd spent with Rochelle in her cottage.

And it was her cottage. Her father had explained after her graduation ceremony that Gran had promised it to her and her mother, after Rochelle graduated, but after her mother's death, the cottage in its entirety would pass to Rochelle. Which it had this week.

"Wait, what about Dunstan? Are you…?" Ben burst out.

Dunstan grinned. "Anemone had her first ultrasound this week. It's the most ingenious device that allows you to see a baby actually in the womb! Or in our case, both babies — we're having twins! What with the risk of what happened last time, I can't let sunlight stop me from protecting her if she needs me. It was almost like magic — one night, I made the decision to do anything it took to break the curse, and the next morning, it was gone!"

"So, is that the reason for this dinner party, then? To celebrate the twins?" Rochelle asked.

Catena shook her head. "The police contacted us this week, regarding their investigation of the basement. You see, there's a law about lost and found items. It usually refers to cash, but the gold in this case is a lot like currency, in that it's almost impossible to trace the owner. If the rightful owner doesn't identify him or herself to claim the currency in question within a particular period of time, then apparently it's finders keepers for whoever found it."

"Now, we all know Ben found it, but because we had to tell the police it was us instead, and we own the property…officially, all that gold now belongs to me and Catena," Anemone said. She held up a hand when Ben opened his mouth to protest. "I know that's not fair, and God knows I don't need it, but it's a great deal of money, so it's not like you can just cash the gold in and tuck the notes into your wallet. You'd need a bank account and proper identification and that kind of money gets noticed, which is why I propose we divide it into six shares, and form a trust. Perhaps we can cash in some of the gold, and place the rest in safe deposit at a bank. That's what we're here to discuss."

Five heads nodded, but Rochelle looked lost. "What gold are you talking about?"

Ben grimaced. He might have forgotten to mention that part. "The butcher turned us into gargoyles to protect a heap of gold he'd stolen from what I believe is the goldfields in Victoria. When I confronted him about it, he only said two words – Nelson, and Williamstown, neither of which were the names of any of the goldfields towns. Unless Nelson was a man…"

In a moment, Rochelle, Catena and Anemone had their phones out, swiping furiously.

Anemone let out a whoop. "Got it! The Nelson was a ship, lying offshore at Williamstown in 1852, when eight thousand ounces of gold or thereabouts was stolen from it, and never recovered. The owner at the time was…the British government, and their present Prime Minister is too much of an idiot to notice anything going on over here. No wonder no one tried to claim it."

Rochelle paled. "Eight thousand ounces? That's…what's that in metric measurements? Not that it matters. At the current price of gold, that's…"

"More than twenty million dollars," Anemone said. "More than any one person needs, which is why I propose we share it. Of course, you boys will need to procure some sort of identity documents…I wouldn't know where to start with such things, though."

Rochelle looked thoughtful. "I'm sure Octavia will know someone. I'll ask her when I see her next."

More nodding. They quickly hashed out the details as they finished their dinner, and they'd reached an agreement before dessert.

When Rochelle carried in the cake she'd bought from the café, she found the brothers deep in discussion.

"You know, it's funny. Father filled our head with dreams about how we'd be rich men once we came to the Swan River Colony, but the idea wasn't his. It was from Mother's brother, Uncle Stanley, that he caught the Swan River fever. Uncle Stanley and several other men from Mother's family went over with the first colonists. We received one letter from him, telling Father to apprentice us into building trades and to make sure that we could sail and farm, for such skills were sorely needed in the colony, and then nothing. I tried asking about him when we came here, but no one had heard of Stanley Steel," Dunstan said.

Ben shrugged. "I was too young to remember."

Tor laughed. "Indeed! I don't think you were even born yet. I remember promising Uncle Stanley that I would build him a castle in the colony when I arrived. I wonder what happened to him."

Anemone leaned in. "We could try searching for him like we did for Ben. At least we might be able to find what cemetery he was buried in."

Catena's eyes lit up. "Ooh, Alethia's company has just started excavating one of the earliest colonial cemeteries in East Perth. I bet she'll know where to look! And she's giving a presentation at the university tomorrow, along with the archaeologists working on the prison commissariat. I'd planned to go and I figured you might, too." She nodded at Anemone. "Why don't we all go, and you boys can ask her yourselves?"

Ben looked askance at Rochelle.

She shrugged. "Sure, why not?"

SEVENTY-ONE

Dunstan fought not to fall asleep during the presentations. Lots of people talking, using big words, describing bits of bone and even nail clippings as though they were buried treasure. If Anemone and the other lady scholars hadn't been so interested, he would never have agreed to go.

Suddenly, Anemone dug her elbow into his ribs. "Go on!" she whispered.

Dunstan focussed on the stage at the front of the room.

"Any questions?" the woman with the microphone asked.

Dunstan raised his hand. "If you were looking for an ancestor, someone who might have been buried in that cemetery, where would you suggest I start looking?"

The microphone passed to a girl who didn't look much older than Ben. "If you come to see me afterwards, I can give you the details of the records I'd suggest you search through first. We used the same method to determine our excavation plans for the Bronte Street site. Even if there is no gravestone remaining, we still might be able to identify the spot where your ancestor is buried. If he was a Scotman like yourself, maybe I'll get to see him as part of our excavation, or his skeleton, at least."

Polite laughter followed this remark.

Dunstan frowned. "I don't want his bones. I want to know what happened to him!"

Anemone hushed him. "If we find out when he died and where he was buried, it's a start. I mean, all we have is the name of the ship he arrived on and the date at present. If you really want to know your ancestor's final resting place, get that information from her, and I'll help you."

When the talking was over and people began to wander over to the buffet, Dunstan marched up to the girl. Unfortunately, another man had reached her first, so he had to wait.

Glaring daggers at the other man's back didn't seem to do him any damage at all. If anything, it only made the man monopolise the girl for longer.

Finally, he stepped to the side, and bowed to the girl. Then he turned to leave.

Dunstan's heart dropped into his boots as he came face to face with the man, who was the spitting image of… "Uncle Stanley?" he croaked.

ABOUT THE AUTHOR

Demelza Carlton has always loved the ocean, but on her first snorkelling trip she found she was afraid of fish.

She has since swum with sea lions, sharks and sea cucumbers and stood on spray drenched cliffs over a seething sea as a seven-metre cyclonic swell surged in, shattering a shipwreck below.

Demelza now lives in Perth, Western Australia, the shark attack capital of the world.

The *Ocean's Gift* series was her first foray into fiction, followed by her suspense thriller *Nightmares* trilogy. She swears the *Mel Goes to Hell* series ambushed her on a crowded train and wouldn't leave her alone.

Want to know more? You can follow Demelza on Facebook, Twitter, YouTube or her website, Demelza Carlton's Place at:

www.demelzacarlton.com

Books by Demelza Carlton

Siren of Secrets series
Ocean's Secret (#1)
Ocean's Gift (#2)
Ocean's Infiltrator (#3)

Siren of War series
Ocean's Justice (#1)
Ocean's Widow (#2)
Ocean's Bride (#3)
Ocean's Rise (#4)
Ocean's War (#5)
How To Catch Crabs

Nightmares Trilogy
Nightmares of Caitlin Lockyer (#1)
Necessary Evil of Nathan Miller (#2)
Afterlife of Alana Miller (#3)

Mel Goes to Hell series
The Devil's Work (#1)
See You in Hell (#2)
Mel Goes to Hell (#3)
To Hell and Back (#4)
The Holiday From Hell (#5)
All Hell Breaks Loose (#6)
The Devil Goes to Heaven (#7)

Romance Island Resort series

Maid for the Rock Star (#1)
The Rock Star's Email Order Bride (#2)
The Rock Star's Virginity (#3)
The Rock Star and the Billionaire (#4)
The Rock Star Wants A Wife (#5)
The Rock Star's Wedding (#6)
Maid for the South Pole (#7)

Romance a Medieval Fairytale series

Enchant: Beauty and the Beast Retold
Dance: Cinderella Retold
Fly: Goose Girl Retold
Revel: Twelve Dancing Princesses Retold
Silence: Little Mermaid Retold
Awaken: Sleeping Beauty Retold
Embellish: Brave Little Tailor Retold
Appease: Princess and the Pea Retold
Blow: Three Little Pigs Retold
Return: Hansel and Gretel Retold
Wish: Aladdin Retold
Melt: Snow Queen Retold
Spin: Rumpelstiltskin Retold
Kiss: Frog Prince Retold
Reflect: Snow White Retold
Roar: Goldilocks Retold
Cobble: Elves and the Shoemaker Retold
Float: Enchanted Horse Retold
Steal: Forty Thieves Retold
Call: Pied Piper Retold
Feather: Swan Maidens Retold

Curse: Rose Red Retold
Cross: Three Billy Goats Gruff Retold
Weave: Rapunzel Retold
Claim: Puss in Boots Retold

Colony Universe
Cowboys and Aliens
Ghost
Vulcan
Cupid
Valentine
Prometheus
Halcyon
Poseidon
Apollo

Heart of Stone series
Broken Chains
Broken Bonds
Broken Dreams

Heart of Steel series
Stone Guardian
Stone Champion
Stone Sentinel
Stone Shadow

www.ingramcontent.com/pod-product-compliance
Lightning Source LLC
Chambersburg PA
CBHW072007180726
48291CB00001BA/163